Love ~~NOTEBOOK~~

feelings are forever

Love
~~A~~ NOTEBOOK

feelings are forever

amber vane

■SCHOLASTIC

Scholastic Children's Books
An imprint of Scholastic Ltd
Euston House, 24 Eversholt Street
London, NW1 1DB, UK
Registered office: Westfield Road, Southam, Warwickshire, CV47 0RA
SCHOLASTIC and associated logos are trademarks and
or registered trademarks of Scholastic Inc.

First published as *I Taught Him a Lesson He'll Never Forget* by
Scholastic Publications Ltd, 1998
This edition published in the UK by Scholastic Ltd, 2009

Text copyright © Amber Vane, 1998

ISBN 978 1407 11155 1

British Library Cataloguing-in-Publication Data
A CIP catalogue record for this book is available from the British Library

The right of Amber Vane to be identified as the author
of this work has been asserted by her.

Printed in the UK by CPI Bookmarque, Croydon, CR0 4TD
Papers used by Scholastic Children's Books are made
from wood grown in sustainable forests.

1 3 5 7 9 10 8 6 4 2

www.scholastic.co.uk/zone

Prologue

P *lease don't die! Please don't die!* The words keep
pounding through my head like a drum, my whole
being aching with dread and anguish. Once more I get up and
pace the long, bare hospital corridor, my shoes squeaking on
the harsh linoleum floor. Why are they taking so long? How
can they leave me like this – not knowing, not having any idea
what's going on behind that closed door?

I glance at my watch for the millionth time. 9.33 p.m. Just
three minutes since I last checked. But each minute, each
second is creeping by so slowly. Have you any idea what it
feels like to come face to face with tragedy, knowing that
everything has been your own fault? Can you imagine what
it's like to kill someone and then only regret it when it's too
late? Well, that's what's happening to me now. That's why
time is crawling by, each moment another needle of torture as
I wait to discover how many lives I've destroyed . . .

1

One

I'm not the girl I used to be. And I'm beginning to wonder if I ever really knew who she was anyway. I look back now at everything that's happened as if that girl was a stranger. How I ever could have thought those thoughts and done those things? One moment I was calm, organized, efficient – even dull. The next I was a woman obsessed . . .

It all began just a few short months ago, not long after I started work. I'd left school the summer before without much hope of getting a job. We were all in the same boat, really – too many of us coming out of one little Midlands town, Kirfield, that simply didn't have enough jobs to go round. But unlike many of the others in my year, I was willing to move away. More than willing, actually.

You see, my mum and dad weren't like other parents. Dad never talked to me, not like other dads. It was as if from as far back as I could remember he'd been bored with the whole

3

idea of me. Mum made up for it, though. She talked incessantly, but usually it was to harangue me for being such a plain, dull, awkward, useless daughter. It wasn't just that she wasn't supportive, it seemed as if she was out to put me down.

"I don't hold with all this modern nonsense about child-rearing," she'd say. "Discipline is what children need, not spoiling. Don't want you getting any fancy ideas above your station, my girl."

She'd say this so often I began to think it was her religion. She had a horror of being seen to give in to me, so whenever I asked for anything – a bicycle, for instance, or a birthday party, or permission to go baby-sitting – she automatically said no. In the end I more or less gave up asking.

The result was that I grew to share my parents' view of myself. I thought I was useless and plain and awkward – and not worth bothering with. I was forced to finish every scrap of every meal my mother dumped in front of me – usually rather nasty, overcooked, fatty food – so I was overweight and lumpy. And I was never allowed to wear fashionable clothes: Mum thought it would give me airs and graces. "And anyway, you'd just look a fright, with your figure."

I found it difficult to make friends. How could I expect anyone to like me when I didn't even like myself? And I hadn't any brothers or sisters to play with. I was the focus of all my mum's disapproval and my dad's coldness. It wasn't even as if they had much time for each other, either. They didn't talk much and they certainly never touched. I grew up never seeing my parents kissing or holding hands or having a laugh together.

By the time I'd done my A levels I was ready to get out – more than ready. So when I saw the ad for an assistant for a firm of estate agents way over at Dudlace, a good fifty miles from where we lived, I jumped at it. And to my amazement, they jumped at me. Maybe my A level in Computer Studies had something to do with it. They said that IT skills were really important, but they also said I seemed mature and efficient, just what they were looking for. And that surprised me, because no one had ever seemed that impressed by me before.

It was just after Christmas when I packed my suitcase – there really wasn't much to take – and moved into my tiny little bedsit, above an Indian restaurant right in the middle of town. It wasn't exactly luxury, but it suited me fine, even though it was so small that I had to fold up the sofa bed each morning just to make enough space to get out to the kitchenette to make my coffee.

It wasn't as if I was expecting visitors. Like I said, I'd never had that many close friends. There was Rebecca, the nearest I'd got to a best friend. We used to walk to school together and sit next to each other up to GCSEs, but then she'd gone and got pregnant, and then got married. We still saw each other occasionally but somehow it was never the same. And as for boyfriends? Well, that just hadn't happened either.

So I was quite content with my new, cosy little home. It was very tidy and clean, just the way I liked it, and very convenient – I could even walk to work. And that was the best thing of all: from the very first day, I absolutely loved my job at Cherry and Simpkins. I was supposed to work for the two directors, Tom Cherry and Margaret Simpkins, but there were also four young agents who were so disorganized that I could tell at once I'd be clearing up after them too. And I didn't mind. It was good to feel useful, and they were certainly appreciative.

"Where's that new list from the Summerfield estate?" Jake yelled over the desk.

Silently, I handed it to him. He snatched it with a frown.

"Looks different. What've you done with it?"

I blushed. "Oh, it came in a bit messy so I thought I'd retype it. I've added a sort of star system to indicate prices, and those numbers are bedrooms."

"Very nice," whistled Alex, looking over Jake's shoulder. "Reminds me of the way I rate football teams."

"Me, too," I admitted, blushing even more.

And it was true. Football was my big weakness, my passion.

I'd spend hours making out charts and lists, organizing fixtures, putting my favourite squads in interminable new formations.

"This is based on the one I did for the European Cup a few years ago, except that it doesn't actually work quite as well for houses."

"Yes, it does," said Alex, scrutinizing my list more closely. "I think you're on to something, Katie, I really do. I mean, these great big ugly double-fronted Victorian jobs are obviously the goalies, and the end-of-terrace semis have got to be wingers . . ."

And he was off, turning all the houses on the list into football stars until we were all falling about laughing.

"What's that mark meant to be?" he demanded, jabbing his finger at a brown stain on the corner of the page.

"Oh dear," said Sarah, who'd just got back from lunch. "I'm afraid that's where I spilt my Diet Coke."

"No problem," I said. "I'll just print off another one."

They were all so grateful, it made me feel really good. For the first time in my life I was needed – and best of all I loved that sense of belonging, of really fitting in. I'd never been very good at socializing and I was dreadful at parties. I was so shy and so awful at small-talk that I usually ended up in the kitchen, washing glasses or clearing up plates. I know it sounds pathetic, but you don't know what it was like being me – not all that pretty, unless you counted my blue eyes which were OK, and my thick black hair which my mum always made me wear in a ponytail.

She was old-fashioned, my mum. She never could understand why girls squandered so much money on clothes, for instance. So when everyone else went rushing out to buy trendy new stuff for parties and clubs, I usually had to make do with horrible old stuff, which was practically always too long, too loose and totally uncool.

So I was really beginning to enjoy my new life and especially all that freedom. Especially when, one Friday, just as I was closing down my computer, Sarah stopped at my desk.

"Hey, Katie, we're off to the pub for a quick end-of-the-week drink. Fancy coming along?" And she gave me this lovely friendly smile, as if she really wanted me to join them.

I grinned back and said that'd be great, as casually as I could, even though I was feeling quite nervous. I'd never even been in a pub before. And I was so shy! Even though I'd blown far too much of my first pay packet on some really tight black jeans and a skimpy top, even though I had my own place and was in charge of my own life, I was still me inside: uptight, lonely, unsure of myself and socially hopeless.

But I needn't have worried. It was just so easy being with the gang from work. We had a game of darts and no one seemed to mind that I was so awful at it that I nearly impaled the pub cat against the wall. Alex just laughed his head off and said he'd have to give me some personal tuition.

He came and stood right beside me, his arm round my shoulders so that he could guide my throwing hand.

"Just keep your eye on the board," he instructed me, his mouth very close to my ear. "Concentrate as hard as you can and just let the dart skim out of your hand."

I tried, I really did. But that time the dart flew completely the wrong way and landed on the ceiling. And even then everyone just laughed and said that I had to buy the next round.

Alex came and helped me to carry the drinks back to our table.

"I don't understand how a football fan can be so useless at darts," he said wonderingly. "I thought it was kind of in the blood."

"Well, I'm OK at Subbuteo," I defended myself. "Maybe I'm just a natural flicker."

"You sound like a candle," remarked Alex.

"No, that would be blow-football," I corrected him. "Different game entirely."

He laughed as we slopped the drinks down and squeezed into the little corner seat.

"So what team do you support then?" he asked.

"Definitely Aston Villa," I answered at once. "That's my main team. But in Europe I like Barcelona, worldwide I've a sneaking affection for Argentina most of the time, and when it comes to other UK teams –" I lowered my voice dramatically and looked round the pub as if checking that no one could overhear – "Glasgow Rangers."

"No!" they all howled at once.

And then everyone started arguing about who was Scotland's best, and Sarah said she supported me over Argentina because you couldn't beat their players for gorgeous legs. Amy, the other agent, pointed out that you could these days – you only had to look at Arsenal.

The guys immediately started to change the subject, possibly because all that frank talk about thighs and bottoms left them feeling inadequate. Alex supported Aston Villa, just like me, but Jake scoffed at both of us, clearly preferring Liverpool, which we considered a betrayal. After all, if you come from the Midlands the least you can do is follow a local team.

"Well, what about our local team?" Alex asked.

I looked blank. He explained that Dudlace had a really quite respectable local club who weren't exactly in the big time yet but were about to get a big breakthrough.

"Don't listen to him," Sarah advised. "He's always saying they're about to make it big. It's because he was born here.

10

They sort of feed you all this loyalty stuff when you're still a baby, and then when you grow up you're hooked."

"Which is why you never really grow up," added Amy. "Although, talking of tasty thighs, there is one really big attraction in our squad, you know."

Both girls shouted out: "James Angel!"

Alex looked offended. "You just happen to be talking about the most promising newcomer since David Beckham stormed into the England squad," he announced.

"We were agreeing," Sarah protested, looking hurt. "We were just saying he was a rare bit of talent."

"That's not the same as being unusually talented," said Alex. "It's not just a question of looks, you know." As the girls gave him knowing looks and started giggling, he turned to me and went on earnestly, "You should see him in action, Katie; you really should. He's magic on legs! I've seen him touch the ball, just barely touch it with his ankle, calculating a shot in a split second, and looking as if he's applying no effort at all – just rolling it into the net. You really need to see him in action, Katie. How about coming along with us to the match tomorrow?"

"Count me out," said Sarah. "I can think of better things to do than stand around in the freezing cold in the middle of January, watching all those lovely legs going blue."

"You will," Alex told her confidently. "You always say you

11

won't come and then you always do. Anyhow, there'll be a gang of us, Katie, so why not come along? You'll be astonished, I just know you will."

And he was right, even though he didn't realize quite how right. Not at first, anyhow.

Two

"Go on, Angel! Tackle him, you great big softie! That's it, go for him!"

That was Alex, yelling for all he was worth, standing and roaring away, his face bright red with excitement. His mate Sam was on his feet too, shouting even louder.

"Dudlace! Dudlace! Go for it! Get your feet moving, Dudlace! What are you, ball players or ballerinas?"

Just then, James Angel did a spectacular tackle, got control of the ball and headed it into a beautiful arc all the way to the very far winger, who took it with a back kick, then dribbled a few steps – just a very few steps – while James raced up the centre of the pitch and overtook him. The winger jerked the ball at a practically impossible angle. It was as if the whole crowd was holding its breath at the same time. And then, all together, we burst into a frenzied roar as James Angel took the pass, flipped forward almost like a dancer, and gave a fluid, effortless kick which sent the ball straight past the defence ranged in front of him, somehow straight through them, past a baffled goalie and right into the net.

To my amazement, I found I was screaming along with everyone else. I'd been to dozens of matches before, but never with a gang like this, never with this fabulous feeling of camaraderie and fun. We were all on our feet, screeching and whistling, stamping, waving our scarves and banging our seats.

I hugged Sarah, who was on one side of me. Sam hugged Alex, then Alex hugged me.

"Told you he was worth watching," Alex whispered, his arms still tight round my shoulders.

"You were right," I replied happily. "He's really something. I'm – I'm glad you asked me along, Alex."

"Me, too," he smiled.

His arm tightened round me for just a second longer, and then his attention was back on the pitch. And mine was, too. Every single bit of me was concentrating on the perfect figure of James Angel – built like a footballer but with the face of an actor: sensitive, vulnerable, deeply handsome. I was willing him to score again, to demonstrate even more spectacular finesse and imagination. Of course, I wanted the team to win, but there was something else, too. Something about that delicate, interesting face, the frown as he concentrated on the ball, the grim set of his mouth as he took a penalty. I wanted him to outdo himself because I could tell that he would be in anguish if he didn't. He was that kind of player – hard on himself, unable to take too much disappointment.

How did I know? Well, you can tell a lot about character from a player's technique as well as from his face, his posture, the way he walks. And I could tell right away that this was no ordinary footballer, no ordinary guy. He was special. He was good.

"You seem thoughtful," Alex commented as we piled into the nearest café after the match for some coffee and doughnuts. "Not too upset about the score, I hope."

I grinned. Dudlace had won 4–1. Angel had scored two of the goals and set up another. It was a good feeling, watching them win, and another good feeling knowing that James Angel must be basking in the glory right now, the hero of the team, striker of strikers.

"I was just thinking how great Angel must be feeling," I said, "knowing how brilliantly he's played."

"No," Sarah put in unexpectedly. "I don't think he's like that at all. I bet he's just not satisfied. There's some move that wasn't quite how he planned it, some detail most people wouldn't even notice. And that's torture for him."

"What makes you say that?" I asked, curious.

"He's a perfectionist," Sam put in, agreeing with Sarah.

"You know what they're like: never satisfied, always striving to be one step ahead." Sam, who was a slightly chubby, slightly short guy with a lovable smile and a laid-back manner, came across as so relaxed that he couldn't possibly understand what it must be like to be driven and obsessive.

"How can you tell, though?" I persisted, intrigued.

"Well, for one thing, I've heard him say so," said Sarah. "On the show."

"What show?" I asked, feeling bewildered.

"He's got his own show on the local radio station," Alex explained. "It's a football phone-in on Radio Dudlace. Every Monday night. You should tune in some time, Katie; he's quite good."

"Yeah, but he had to have a load of training for it," Sam added. "My mate William's the producer down there. He said James was dead nervous to begin with. They had to give him loads of practice."

"Hard to believe," said Sarah. "He sounds really natural. Like a friend."

"Well, he does now," Sam said knowingly, "but it took a while."

"You're just jealous," Amy teased him. "Bet you couldn't host a radio show."

"Bet you couldn't beat me at darts," retorted Sam.

"Beat you?" Amy scoffed. "I could slaughter you more like!"

And somehow, everyone agreed we'd meet up later on at the pub for a grand match.

"How about you, Katie?" Alex asked. "You coming?"

I smiled nervously. "Er . . . well, I don't think anyone will want me on their team if it's going to be a darts night," I said, remembering my embarrassing attempts the night before.

"Oh, come on, Katie!" they urged. "You'll improve with practice."

So I did. And once again, I had a really good time. They were all so good-natured and friendly. Sam's girlfriend came along too. She was a secretary, like me, which was a bit of a relief. I was worried about being with all these people I worked for. It was hard to believe I was really welcome, but Holly was one of the gang, so why shouldn't I be, too?

"You know, I'm really glad you've come," Alex said, bringing me a drink. "I don't just mean that you've come out tonight. I mean I'm glad you've come to Dudlace – and to work with us."

"Me, too," I answered shyly. "I never dreamed it'd work out so well."

Alex gave me a long, appraising look then, staring at me for so long that I wondered whether I had a peanut stuck to my chin or something.

"Why do you always wear your hair in that ponytail?" he asked at last.

Surprised, I shrugged. "I dunno – I've always done it this way."

"What's it like when you let it loose?" he asked.

Obediently, I reached behind my head, pulled off the band and shook out my thick black hair. Everyone gathered round to stare at me.

"Wow!" said Sam. "You look . . . different."

"You look great," corrected Alex, staring at me even more closely.

I wasn't used to being looked at, to being the centre of attention. I could feel my face burning.

"Fabulous hair," Sarah commented approvingly. "But you know what? I think you'd look great with a bob."

"Even shorter," nodded Amy. "You've got great features, Katie. You could cut it right up to the neck and you'd look really striking."

I was too embarrassed to speak at all. Luckily, Holly must have understood how difficult it was for me to be scrutinized by everyone like this.

"Oh, leave her alone," she said good-humouredly. "You're all jealous because she's got such lovely long hair. I wish mine was thick and shiny like that." Holly had amazing curly blonde hair, so I knew she was only saying that to rescue me and I was grateful.

But even so, I'd had enough for one night.

"Better get off home," I announced as soon as I'd finished my drink. "Bye, everyone!" And even though I left them all still crowded round the darts board enjoying themselves, I didn't feel left out or lonely. I felt good – really good. Maybe things were looking up for me at last . . .

Over the next few weeks, my life slipped into a happy routine. On Friday evening, I usually went out with the gang after work for a drink. On Saturdays, we'd go and see Dudlace if they were playing at home. If not, I might go out with Holly, who was turning into a good friend. Sometimes the whole gang would meet up for a pizza after the match and, just occasionally, it would be just me and Alex. He was getting to be quite a good mate, too, although I didn't really believe he could want to go out with me. I was getting a little more confident, but I had a way to go . . .

Anyway, every Monday I had a really hot date – with the radio. I listened avidly to James Angel's football show. It was the highlight of the week. He had the most gorgeous velvety voice, quite unlike what you'd expect from a football player. And he was funny too, always telling little stories about disasters that happened behind the scenes, or else making rude comments about the big league players.

After about a month, two things happened. The first was that Alex invited me to go and see Aston Villa playing at home to Norwich. It was a perfect day – really perfect. Although it was still only February, it was bright and sunny, almost like spring. We drove to Birmingham in Alex's beat-up Metro, listening to CDs.

The game was OK – not brilliant but pretty satisfying to watch because Villa slaughtered the visitors with a resounding 2–0 score which was only made a little less than wonderful because the second was an own-goal by a new player. And I was sorry for him. Call me a great big softie, but that's the way I am.

Maybe it didn't seem so exciting after all those Dudlace matches. Obviously, watching a Premier League game is a different experience. The expertise is there, for a start, and the ground is so much more vast. It's all on a different scale. But the raw edge of excitement was missing, somehow – the feeling that this little local team might any day start to break into the big time, that any one of its players might end up kicking for England . . .

So it wasn't a spectacular match or anything, but it was a great day because of Alex. I just really enjoyed being with him. He wasn't all that good-looking, really. He wore these quite thick glasses that made his green eyes look very big and earnest, and he was a bit skinny, so that the suits he wore at work drooped round his shoulders, and the big black jumper he always seemed to wear for football matches flopped too far down his legs. But he was nice – really nice. And he seemed to care about me.

After the match we wandered round town for a bit, and then went for a curry right in the heart of town. It was quite late by the time we'd driven the fifty or so miles back to Dudlace and he'd drawn up outside my flat. He turned towards me, leaned over and brushed his lips gently against mine.

"Thanks for a great day," he said softly. "We must do it again some time."

"Er . . . yes," I replied, my lips still tingling. "Thanks. Thanks, Alex."

I was too confused, too overcome to say anything more sensible. I still couldn't quite believe he'd actually asked me out. I slipped out of the car, cursing myself for being so awkward and unsure of myself. Probably he'd think I wasn't all that bothered about him. Probably he only wanted to be friends anyway. Probably he'd never ask me out again.

But I was wrong. And actually, the second thing that happened turned out to be far more significant. He greeted me cheerfully when I got to work on Monday, just as if nothing had happened between us. And I thought it very likely that nothing had. Then he stopped by my desk with a huge mountain of contracts.

"Sorry I let these pile up," he said. "I got behind because I mixed up Carlton Road with Carlton Avenue."

"Oh, not again!" chorused the others.

"Honestly, Alex, you're just not safe to have around this office," groaned Sarah.

"I don't mind – I'll sort these out this afternoon," I said.

"Well, don't work too late," Alex warned me. "I've just had a call from Sam, and he's just had a call from his mate William. They want some extra helpers on the phones tonight for James Angel's phone-in. He's doing a special quiz with tickets as prizes, and they reckon they're going to be inundated. Fancy coming along?"

"OK," I said, trying to sound casual. "Sounds fun."

"Good. That makes – how many?" Alex called across the office. "Sarah? Good. Amy? Jake?"

"Nope," Jake said, not looking up from his screen. "Got a date."

"Just the four of us then," said Alex. "Plus Sam and Holly. Should be a laugh."

I turned to my computer, staring hard at the contracts programme I'd just called on to the screen. But I couldn't concentrate. All I could think of was James Angel. I was going to meet James Angel. And all thoughts of Alex – his contracts, the feel of his lips on mine, the eager smile on his face – vanished clean out of my mind.

Three

"The James Angel Show. What's your question, please?" I asked for the twenty-seventh time, scribbling furiously as I tried to take down the latest complicated query.

"Guy wants to see if James can remember the line-up in the Villa squad last time they played Arsenal!" I yelled at once. I knew the producer had been waiting for a Premier League question. Too many so far had been about the local team and had posed no challenge to James at all.

"Great! Call him back fast!" shouted the producer. "And tap his details onto the screen."

Happily, I managed to type and phone at the same time. I was just about to take another flashing call when James typed back on his screen: "Anyone know what month it was?"

Immediately, I was back on the keyboard. "December 2008," I tapped in.

James grinned his thanks as he carried on his seamless

string of chatter to the listeners, each time coming up with even more details than they'd asked for. He was good. The guy was really good.

I'd noticed how gorgeous he was at once, and was aware of it all the way through the frantic activity and rush of the live phone-in show – the bank of telephones flashing and all the helpers rushing around trying to answer them, get information to the producer, log the names of all the callers and even the names of the tracks of CDs that James put on occasionally to keep up the suspense.

Somehow, there was an extra thrill to it all, knowing that all the frenzy and panic was centred round this one compelling figure. Dark-haired, dark-eyed, with a tense jaw and firm-boned cheeks, James was even better-looking than he'd seemed on the football field. He was quite slim but very powerfully built, with a strength in his shoulders that you could almost feel through his white linen shirt, open to reveal a tanned, slightly hairy chest.

But there was no time to stare through the glass. The phones were flashing non-stop and soon I was yelling through another cracking question, this time a bit trickier.

"Who won the 2002 World Cup?" I tapped out, knowing in advance that this was just what the producer was after. "And which side knocked out England in that same competition?"

James looked up, his handsome face creased with

concentration. No, it wasn't just concentration now, it was anxiety. He didn't know! At last the giant was in trouble. Someone was about to win the play-off!

"Well, everyone will remember the answer to that one," he told the caller, sounding completely unruffled. Meanwhile, he was tapping wildly on his screen: HELP!

He was stalling, I could tell. I had to help him. Furiously, I tapped away into the computer.

"The World Cup was won that year by Brazil, two-nil against Germany," James went on, squinting at the screen. "And for the second part of your question . . ."

His face lit up as he read my message on his screen. Effortlessly, he continued: "England was knocked out by Brazil – in the quarter-finals . . ."

"Well done, Katie!" said the producer, William, tapping me on the back. "I reckon you've saved all our skins tonight. Our James doesn't exactly enjoy being caught out, you know."

I glowed with pride and pleasure. I could hardly believe this was happening to me. Katie Wakefield, plain, dumpy, shy, awkward – could this really be the same girl? Here I was, surrounded by a bunch of people who actually seemed to enjoy having me around. And now I was working on a radio programme, not just enjoying myself but actually helping and making people grateful. It was a new feeling, but I thought I could probably get used to it . . .

25

James was just finishing the show, congratulating all the listeners on being great sports, telling them it was them who made the show really, not him. And he even picked a few names out of a hat to be winners, since no one had actually managed to catch him out for the whole two hours.

Triumphantly, he whipped off his headphones, strode out of his studio and came to join us in the crowded, bustling studio.

"Thanks, team," he said, his tense face breaking into a sudden smile. He clapped his hands over the producer's shoulders. "Great going, William – well done. And this lot were on form tonight. I reckon we should do these bonanzas more often, with back-up like this. Hey, let's all go to the pub now. They've kept that private room for me . . ."

"You're looking good tonight, Katie," Sarah commented, as we squeezed into the tiny ladies' room and lined up by the mirror to do our lipstick. "It's your hair, isn't it? You should wear it loose more often. It's fabulous like that – all thick and wild. Here – you should try some red lipstick, pink's too pale for you."

I took the stick of bright scarlet lipstick she offered and applied it gingerly.

"Not like that," Sarah said impatiently. "Here, let me do it." She drew bold, heavy lines over my lips, then handed me a tissue to blot them.

I peeped at the mirror and gulped, amazed at how different I looked. The lipstick made me look bold and fiery – not at all like me.

Sarah gazed at me critically. "Don't you ever wear blusher?" she demanded. "Here, try mine." And before I could protest she was brushing red powder across my cheekbones, making me look even more wanton.

"Good," she said. "Suits her, doesn't it?" Holly and Amy nodded approvingly.

"You've lost weight, haven't you?" Holly added.

I was too embarrassed to answer, but I knew she was right. Away from Mum's old-fashioned, starchy cooking I was eating healthier food, and far less of it. I was too busy to think about food, and I certainly never bothered with chocolate any more. Just this evening, while I was getting ready to come out, I'd glanced at myself in the mirror and noticed how much smaller my waist seemed to be. The waistband was loose, even though my jeans were quite new.

"You should show off that figure of yours, you know, Katie," Holly told me. "I mean, that jumper's OK and everything, but it's not exactly – well . . ."

"What are you wearing underneath?" demanded Amy.

"Er . . . my vest," I muttered, blushing even redder than my newly made-up cheeks.

"Let's see," chorused the girls. Overcome with confusion I

reluctantly pulled the jumper over my head to reveal a skimpy black vest that barely covered my bra.

"Perfect!" they declared. "That's just right!"

"But I can't go to a party in my underwear," I protested.

"Course you can," scoffed Sarah. "Who's going to notice?"

"You look really cool now," Holly consoled me. "And at least it goes with your jeans."

So it was a very new me who emerged into the crowded room, heaving with people chatting, laughing, all crushed up against each other. Holly was right, I thought. My vest looked very much like the tight little tops that most of the girls were wearing. So I stopped feeling quite so self-conscious, especially when a familiar voice beside me whispered: "You look amazing, Katie!"

It was Alex. I turned to smile at him. I'd barely seen him all evening, everyone had been so busy. He handed me a glass of wine, then clinked his with mine.

"Cheers!" he said. "Glad you could make it tonight."

We were chatting away happily, laughing at some story of Alex's about his latest mix-up at work, when someone tapped me on the shoulder. I turned round and it was all I could do to stop myself from gasping. There before me was the man himself – James Angel. And he was looking straight into my eyes.

"Excuse me," he said politely to Alex, then turned back to

me with that full, intense gaze. "You're Katie Wakefield, aren't you?"

I nodded.

"You were the one who got me out of that hole tonight, weren't you?" he went on. "Oh, and I enjoyed the message. *England lost to Brazil. Love, Katie.*"

This time I blushed so hard I thought I might burst into flames. "I didn't put that did I?"

He grinned. "You did. And I thought it was charming. Of course, I mostly thought that because you were right. And come to think of it, you must have been the one who added the information about Villa v. Arsenal."

I nodded again. He looked intrigued.

"Well, why haven't I met you before?" he wanted to know. "You're gorgeous, you're sexy – and you know your football."

Just then, the jukebox was turned up, and somehow people managed to move back to make a space on the floor.

"Dance?" James suggested. His arm touched my elbow and steered me into the middle.

I was quaking with terror. I couldn't dance. I'd never been able to. And here I was, with the most attractive man in the room, the centre of everyone's attention – about to make a complete fool of myself.

But, somehow, I didn't. The song was *Use Somebody* by Kings of Leon, but a new version. It was slow and romantic

29

and with James's strong arms round me, his body guiding me in time to the music, I found myself floating round the room, almost as if we were one being.

The rest of the evening passed like some amazing dream. James was so easy to get on with and we had so much to talk about. We chatted about football at first, but soon he was asking me about my job and how I came to be in Dudlace, and instead of being tongue-tied as usual I found it was the most natural thing in the world to tell him about myself and to ask him lots of questions, too.

We talked, then danced, then talked some more. And then the jukebox began to play my completely favourite song of all time: *Halo*, by Beyoncé. James drew me towards him and we swayed together, almost embracing in time to the music. His hands were on my waist, very lightly, but just the feel of them was enough to make me melt against his strong, muscular shoulders, wanting this perfect moment to go on for ever, wanting the music to play until dawn.

When it finally faded into the last few bars he pulled me closer towards him, his hands tracing a line up and down my spine.

"Katie," he whispered very gently.

I raised my head to look up at him, and he kissed me. The feel of his lips on mine sent a charge right through me and I knew I was trembling.

He could feel it, too. He held my face steady, cupping my chin in both hands, and kissed me again.

"I want to see you again, Katie," he said softly. "How about Saturday night?"

I nodded mutely, unable to believe my luck. James Angel had asked me out! James Angel wanted to see me again!

"Told you the vest was a good idea," Holly teased me as we all wandered out into the night. "You lucky thing!"

The girls were dying to know what he'd said to me, what had happened. But somehow it was just too precious to talk about. So I was quiet on the way home, while all the others were laughing and chattering. Only Alex seemed a bit subdued, but there wasn't much I could do about that. James Angel had asked me out, after all.

Four

I was ready a whole hour before James was due to pick me up that Saturday night. In fact, I'd spent all day getting ready, and most of the previous week thinking about the big date and planning it.

I'd blown nearly a week's salary on a new outfit: an outrageously short black velvet dress and flirty little black strappy shoes to match. I'd never dared wear anything like it before, but with my new, growing confidence and my new slim figure everything seemed possible somehow.

I'd spent most of the afternoon in the bathroom. I gave myself a facial, painted my nails – even my toenails – washed and conditioned my hair and experimented with more make-up than I'd worn in my whole life up till now.

By six o'clock I was dressed and raring to go. At six-fifteen I thought I'd try something different with my hair and spent ages making loads of tiny plaits and finishing them off with coloured beads. At seven o'clock I decided it looked awful and abandoned the whole thing. In the end, I left it loose and wild, but added some sparkly ear-rings which flashed just occasionally when I tossed my head. That was it. I was ready and waiting. And as petrified as if I was about to go on stage to sing the lead role in *Madame Butterfly*.

I sat staring into space, sipping a lemonade and making myself more and more nervous. At exactly eight o'clock the doorbell rang, startling me so much that my drink flew into the air and sprayed all over me. I rushed to the bathroom to dab myself dry, relieved that I hadn't been drinking coffee or, even worse, Coke. Then I'd probably smell funny . . . oh, no! Perfume! I'd nearly forgotten! Wildly, I rummaged in the bathroom cabinet for my new bottle of Chanel No. 5 – so wildly that all the jars and packets and bottles tumbled out on to the floor.

By the time I opened the front door I was practically hyperventilating. I'd taken so long I was sure James must have given up and gone home. And I almost hoped he had, I felt so flustered and anxious. Besides, I was also smelling like the entire perfume floor at Harrods. He was bound to hate me.

But the minute I opened the door all my nerves disappeared. James was leaning against the doorpost, grinning lazily at me. He looked gorgeous, his deep blue eyes accentuated by the blue and green Ben Sherman shirt he was wearing under a very casual but obviously expensive black leather jacket.

"Wow!" he said, taking in my new, glam look. "Love the dress! But . . . erm . . . I hope you weren't expecting dinner at the Ritz or anything."

Oh no! I thought. I've overdone it. He's looking casual and I'm all dressed up! But I managed to grin and shrug.

"Wherever . . . I'd probably wear this if we were just staying in to catch up on Match of the Day. Provided it was with you . . ."

There was no mistaking the appreciation in his eyes – not just of the way I looked, but of my bold come-on. I could hardly believe it was me flirting like this, but it seemed to be going down a treat.

James's car was surprisingly modest – a four-year-old Fiesta, nothing flashy at all. I was quite pleased about that. It made me feel as if I was more in his league, somehow. And he took me to a nice but fairly ordinary pasta restaurant in town, which was a huge relief, as I'd been worrying about what I'd do if we went somewhere fancy and I had to work out how to eat mussels or cope with artichokes.

Best of all, though, was how easy it was to be with him. The whole evening was magical. We chatted away like old friends, discovering more and more that we had in common.

"I love *Batman*, don't you?" James confided.

"Especially *The Dark Knight*. That was the best movie I've ever seen, definitely."

"*Batman*'s cool, but James Bond is the best! Daniel Craig in *Quantum of Solace* is something else! I even bought the dvd, I loved it so much."

"Hmm," James teased. "And there we were, getting on so well. I knew there had to be a catch. OK let's do female stars. Who's your favourite?"

"Rebecca Hall in *Vicky Cristina Barcelona*, but otherwise Scarlett Johansson in practically anything," I replied instantly. If there was something I really did know about, it was films. That's what comes of spending all your weekends stuck at home watching dvds.

"Interesting," James remarked, gazing at me in a way that made my stomach do little aerobics routines inside me. "Great looking, great tastes, great appetite." He looked at my plate. I'd managed to finish my entire pizza and salad without even realizing it. I blushed. This was so embarrassing!

James put his hand on mine. "No, don't go all coy," he said gently. "I hate it when you take out a girl and she can't even finish her food. It's so boring. Now you – you're obviously an enjoyer."

'What do you mean?" I asked, intrigued.

"Well, there are people who enjoy life and people who are scared of it," he explained.

I thought fleetingly of my normal self – the one who was afraid of meeting people, afraid of new experiences, afraid of practically everything. But that was the old me. This flamboyant woman with the mass of black hair, the tiny dress, the scarlet lipstick, putting away pizza and draining a glass of red wine – that was the new me. Adventurous. Ready for anything.

I clinked my glass with his. "I'll drink to that!" I said, gazing boldly back into his eyes. "Wow, we've finished our glasses!"

"Well, I'd love to order another but I'm driving," James said.

So it seemed only natural for us to go back to his place, where he had a whole bottle waiting in the fridge.

James's flat was a bit like his car – comfortable without being expensive or flashy. Trophies and cups lined his shelves and his mantelpiece. One whole wall was covered with framed photographs, some of them action shots of James, some of famous big league matches, and one or two of James shaking hands with famous footballers like Beckham and Joe Cole. I flopped into a big, squashy sofa and gazed round with interest. There was so much to look at.

James appeared with a glass of chilled wine for each of us, and sat on the sofa very close to me.

"Cheers," he said softly, and we clinked glasses. But I'd

barely taken my first sip before he reached over and removed the glass from my hand.

Expertly, he pulled me towards him and kissed me, gently at first and then more insistently, his lips scorching mine and sending wild flames licking right through me.

Feeling my response, he moved away from me for just a moment and gave me a long, slow look. Then, without speaking, he lowered me down on to the sofa, and as he kissed me again his hands travelled up and down the soft velvet of my dress, pressing my waist and hips then moving up and down again with insistent caresses that made my whole being melt at his touch.

I gasped with shock and pleasure at the sensations that were coursing through my body. I'd never felt anything so powerful, so overwhelming, in my whole life. Now James was lying on top of me, the weight of his body crushing mine. My head was flung back in abandon as his mouth burned into my neck, my throat, then back on to my lips.

My arms were twined round his neck, my body arching towards him, wanting him closer and closer, wanting more than anything to belong to him utterly.

"Oh my God, Katie!" he murmured, his voice harsh with longing. "You are – you're fantastic! And I want you so much . . ."

Then he was kissing me again, his lips bruising mine, his

underneath me now, wandering up to my back, my shoulders, setting my skin on fire at the touch of his fingers.

It was only when he tore off his shirt and gently began unzipping my dress that the alarm bells began to ring. It was all happening much too fast. I was being swept along on this great tide of emotion and desire, but now, feeling his hands on my flesh, his naked skin pressing against mine, I was thrown into panic.

"No!" I panted, my whole body tensing up as I tried to push him away.

"Why? What's wrong?" demanded James, his eyes glittering with passion. "Don't you want me, Katie? Because you're certainly acting as if you do.

"Oh, I do, of course I do," I assured him. "But – not now, not yet . . ."

James gave me a strange, disbelieving look, then pulled me towards him for another kiss. "Tell me you don't want me", he whispered, "and I'll stop."

Somehow I managed to summon up all my self-control and pull away from him. "I can't," I said, tears welling up in my eyes. "Not so soon. I'm just not like that, James . . ."

James shrugged. "OK, love, have it your own way," he said casually, every word piercing my heart like a dart.

I wanted so badly to give in to him, to let him make love to me, but I was scared. It was the first time anyone had wanted me like this, the first time I'd been kissed so passionately. I needed time to think, to prepare myself.

"Just give me a little time," I faltered. "We need to get to know each other . . ."

"I know I want you," James said simply, "and you want me, too. But if a girl says no then I'm not going to force her. So I think we'd better say goodnight, don't you? Come on, I'll drive you home."

As we pulled up outside my flat he leaned over and kissed me. "You're sensational, Katie," he whispered. "You're dynamite. And you've got me so wired up I think I'm going to explode." And for a few blissful moments I was melting in his arms, transported by the strength of his desire, the passion of his embrace.

"So – will we see each other again?" I asked shyly, when at last he released me.

'What?" he asked, distracted. "Oh yes, sure."

"I know – why don't you come over to my place?" I plunged on. "I could cook you a meal. I do a mean chilli con carne. Really hot. Shall we say Wednesday?"

"Er . . . no," James answered quickly. "Sorry, love, I won't be able to make it. We're training out of town for a few days. Tell you what – I'll call you later in the week."

And he was gone. All that night I lay tossing and turning in

...nching the pillow to calm my turbulent thoughts, my body on fire with the new sensations that James had aroused in me. Should I have let him make love to me? Or would he respect me all the more for making him wait?

Five

The next few days passed in a dreamy haze of happiness, tinged with odd moments of doubt. I was in love for the very first time. It altered everything: the trees seemed taller, the fruit I bought at the market seemed juicier, the whole world was sweeter. And all because at last I'd found someone who cared about me, someone who made me feel as if I mattered. At last I was part of things instead of an outsider looking in, peering at life with my nose pressed up against the window pane . . .

Then, in my darker moments, I'd wonder whether I'd been right to stop James from making love to me. Had my rejection hurt him? Did he think less of me because of it? But then I told myself not to be so stupid. He was crazy about me. He'd made that plain enough. And then I'd cheer up and fantasize about seeing him again.

Sarah at work was the first to notice. "Hey, Katie," she

one morning, "what's up with you? You've been ever so quiet this week. It couldn't have anything to do with that dreamy date on Saturday night, could it?"

I smiled a secret smile. "Could be," I agreed.

"So what happened, then?" Sarah probed. "Where'd he take you?"

"Are you seeing him again?" demanded Amy.

"Well, he's away this week," I told them, proud to know so much about the private life of James Angel, "but I expect we'll get together at the weekend. We got on really well . . ."

They pestered me for more details but somehow I didn't want to let them in on too many secrets. What had happened between me and James was so very special, somehow, that it seemed wrong to talk about it.

And although I was floating along on this amazing cloud of joy, I was impatient, too – I wanted so badly to be with James again, to feel his arms round me, his body crushing mine. It was a real shame that he had to go away so soon after our first date – the night we fell in love.

He'd been a bit vague about when he'd be back in town. I supposed that was the way it was with football. When you were part of a team you just had to live and breathe the game and go wherever you were needed. He'd said that they were going to do some advanced training at a special ground near Coventry, but he'd be back for the home match on Saturday.

42

I'd hoped that he'd ring me during the week. Sometimes I found myself panicking about it. Had I offended him? Should I have given myself to him straight away, to show I cared? But then I'd remind myself that he was a footballer, on a punishing routine. It must be really hard to find time to phone if you're away from home, tied up in an exhausting training programme with all your team-mates. Luckily for James, I understood all that because I was a real fan. I wasn't just a girlfriend who had to pretend. I knew all about how important it was to keep at it, to push yourself to the limits and always put the game first.

But by the time Friday came and I still hadn't heard from James I began to feel anxious. Suppose something had happened to him? Suppose he wasn't well? Maybe his phone wasn't working? Or what if he'd forgotten my number?

Yes, that must be it, I decided, relieved. After all, we'd only had that one date together, even if I did feel as though I'd known him my whole life. I thought I'd better ring him, just to make sure everything was OK.

So when the rest of the gang were out for lunch, I dialled his number, trembling a little at the prospect of hearing that sexy, caressing voice once again. He answered on the second ring and my heart gave a little leap.

"James, hello! It's Katie here."

There was just a fraction of a pause before he replied.

"... Of course! Good to hear from you," he said, clearly delighted. "Hey, listen – how are you?"

"Oh, I'm fine," I said carefully. "I just wondered, you know, when we were going to get together again. I mean, you've been out of town, and—"

"Yeah – yeah, sure," James said. "I – I was thinking about calling you but—"

"Don't worry," I interrupted eagerly. "I realized you'd probably forgotten to write down my number. I couldn't remember whether I gave it to you or not. But it doesn't matter now, does it?"

"Er . . . no," he agreed. "Exactly. That's right. Well, look – how about a drink tomorrow night after the match?"

"That'd be perfect," I sighed happily. "Absolutely perfect." And right then I knew exactly what was going to happen. This time we were going to go all the way: I'd give myself to James as a way of sealing our love, of proving that we truly belonged together.

The pub that night was heaving with people, and every single one of them seemed to be a friend of James's, or else they wanted to get to know him, or needed to ask him something or tell him something. And while I just wished they'd all go away so that I could be alone with him, he seemed to be having the time of his life.

Oh well, I thought, smiling as someone spilt their Coke all over me, that's the way it is if you're a star. And if you're the star's girlfriend, you just have to accept it all. No way was I going to be one of those clingy women who's always nagging to go home, or pulling on a guy's arm as if he's her pet. No, I understood all about what a footballer needed from his girl. And tonight here I was, proving it.

I'm not saying it was easy, though. Far from it. First of all there were all the lads who wanted to buy James pints and hang around, being his mates. And the girls were even worse. Every woman in the pub was eyeing him up – even the ones who were with boyfriends of their own.

I noticed a particularly pushy girl who kept trying to whisper secrets in his ear as she brushed past him. She was quite striking, you had to admit it. She was very thin, with spiky blonde hair, skin-tight trousers and a leather jacket. She seemed to be with a group of people who'd taken over a whole corner to themselves and were piling up mountains of crisps and beer bottles. Whenever she said anything the whole crowd of them roared with laughter. In fact, she was just exactly the kind of girl I used to be so jealous of – sexy, confident, sociable.

Now, though, I could afford to feel superior. I might not be as pretty as her, or as lively, but I had James, didn't I? I was the one he wanted, the one he was going to end up with at the

the evening. Once more, she was whispering something in his ear as she made her way to the bar. He looked uncomfortable. She'd obviously embarrassed him, poor thing. It must be hard to turn people down kindly, I thought, imagining that she must have come on to him in some way and he had to rebuff her. After all, he was with me now.

He didn't say that much to me all evening, but he didn't need to. All that mattered was the odd glance, the occasional squeeze of the hand as he passed me a drink. Who cared what went on between us in public, when what we had in private was so special?

"Fancy a game of darts?" said a familiar voice in my ear. It was Alex! I turned round and grinned at him.

"I didn't know you'd be here," I exclaimed. "I'm with James . . ."

Alex glanced over to where James was roaring with laughter at something one of his mates had just said.

"Really?" Alex said drily. "Well, maybe he wouldn't mind if I borrowed you for a while."

So Alex and I slipped off for a game of darts, and then another. And I think he would have quite liked me to stay for another but I said I really had to get back to my table. James would be wondering where I was.

But the good thing about James was that he wasn't at all

possessive. He gave me a wave as I returned to my seat, almost as if he hadn't noticed I'd been gone.

At last it was time for last orders, and people slowly began to disperse until only a few stragglers were left draining the last drops of their beer. The blonde spiky girl had gone, I noticed with satisfaction. So had Alex.

"Come on, love – I'll take you home," James said, his hand caressing my neck. A warm happiness flowed through me. The long, uncomfortable, noisy evening had been worth it. Now I was going to get James all to myself.

When he drew up outside my flat I didn't waste any time. This was my one chance to show him I really cared for him – that this time I wasn't going to hold back. I slid over towards him until my mouth was very close to his, then I kissed him full on the lips, amazed at my own boldness. For just a few seconds he seemed to be holding back, as if he needed to be sure I wouldn't disappoint him. But then I undid my coat and pressed myself against his chest.

At once, I could feel his response. He groaned a little, then pulled me to him and kissed me back roughly, sending darts of passion piercing through me.

Upstairs in my little bedsit he took me in his arms and kissed me, then held me a little away from him, cupping my face with his hands, his eyes asking the unspoken question. He stroked the hair from my face, then fingered one of my gs. They were little golden footballs, and he stared at them for a while.

I knew I had to find a way to answer him, to let him know that this time there would be no holding back. So, very deliberately, I pulled off the earrings and dropped them to the floor. And then, just as slowly, I pulled my top over my head and stood before him invitingly, willing him to want me.

For a few seconds he stared at me, hypnotized. Then he pulled me towards him, crushing me in the sudden rough passion of his embrace, and we collapsed on to the bed in a frenzy of desire. "Katie, you're a witch!" moaned James. "I just can't get enough of you . . ."

And now at last our bodies were pressed together, and he was making love to me with such power, such passion and yet such control that all I could do was abandon myself to the wild ecstasy that coursed through me as I cried out in sheer joy and triumph and total love.

Afterwards, as I lay in his arms, stroking his chest, I asked shyly, "Why did you try to avoid coming up here with me? Didn't you want to make love?"

James gave me a long, searching stare. "Of course I did, Katie," he sighed. "You know I did. You're irresistible; you must know you are. It's just that I wasn't sure what you wanted, after last time. And I – I hadn't realized you were a virgin."

Relief surged through me. "Yes, that's why I held back last time," I told him happily. "I wanted to be really, really sure before I gave myself to you."

"Er – sure about what?" he asked guardedly.

"That you were the right one," I said, surprised that he needed to ask. "That you loved me and I loved you."

"Now, hang on a moment," James said. "I never said—"

"No, and you don't need to," I assured him. "But I understand. I really do. And I feel the same way."

"Look, Katie," James said, looking uncomfortable. "You know, I think you may have the wrong idea. I mean – this whole thing is going way too fast. I think it's getting out of control."

Of course, I knew exactly what he meant. James was afraid of his feelings, overwhelmed by the strength of his love for me. What could be more natural?

"It's OK," I soothed him. "Don't worry. I know exactly what you mean. I feel the same way."

"You do?" he asked, his brow clearing.

"Yes, of course I do. This feeling between us is pretty overpowering, isn't it?" I went on happily. "No wonder we're finding it a bit scary. But it'll be fine. I mean, this is really special, isn't it?"

"Er . . . well . . ." James hesitated. "You know, I still think it'd be best to slow down."

at's what you want," I agreed placidly. "Who needs to
.n, when our love is so strong?"

"That's not quite what I meant," James said, stroking my
hair and still looking troubled. But I didn't want to hear any
more. We were madly in love, that was all that mattered. And
if he wanted to take it slowly, only see me once or twice a
week instead of every single night – well, that was just fine by
me.

But when the following week crawled by with no word from
James, I began to feel a little anxious. Oh, I knew he loved me.
There was no doubt about that, after that wild night together.
But suppose he really was terrified of the intensity of our
passion? What if he was too scared to carry on?

And so, once again, I waited until everyone else was round
at the sandwich bar on Wednesday lunchtime, and dialled
his number. This time there was no doubt about it. He
sounded guarded, like someone with too much to hide.

"James, it's me, Katie!" I told him breathlessly.

"Oh, hi," he answered. "Katie, listen—"

"No, you listen to me," I said, not giving him a chance to
express his doubts. "I know you're having second thoughts
about us, and I quite understand."

"You do?" he asked, sounding disbelieving.

"Of course I do," I told him, a little more confidently than

I felt. "It's only natural. We don't know each other all that well yet, after all."

"Exactly," he said, sounding happier. "We hardly know each other at all. And I think we really need to cool it a little, don't you? It's all happened far too fast and I don't feel ready—"

"You don't feel ready for all these powerful emotions," I finished for him. "I know; I'm finding it pretty scary, too. I mean, I've never felt like this before either."

"Katie," James interrupted. "That's not quite what I'm trying to tell you."

"What is it, then?" I asked tremulously.

There was a very long silence. Then he said quietly: "Katie, you're a fabulous girl. Really. But I need to be alone right now. Please understand. It's not you, it's me. I need a little space."

"OK," I told him. "Why don't we leave it for a few days? And then we'll talk again."

"Yes, I think that would be best," James answered. "I'll call you soon."

It was amazing how cool and controlled I felt as I put down the phone. I suppose it was because just talking to James filled me with such confidence and happiness. He was my guy. I loved him. I understood him. If space was what he wanted, space he would get. But if he thought he was going to

work this thing out all on his own, then he really
n't know me at all.

James needed me. I knew that. And all I had to do was be
there for him, whether he realized it or not.

Six

"Are you hungry?" I called out in my most alluring, teasing voice. "Darling? Are you starved?"

"Where are you?" James called, an edge in his voice that I knew must be raw lust. "Katie . . . ?"

"Come and find me," I suggested, allowing the faintest laugh to gurgle through my words as I hugged my naked body, nestling between the crisp white sheets of his bed. Oh, he was in for a surprise all right! Any second now he was going to be standing in that doorway, contemplating the treat I was all ready to serve up . . .

I hadn't planned it this way, of course. Well, not exactly. After our last conversation, just a week ago, I'd decided to play it cool for a while. Oh, I had no doubt at all that it was only a matter of time before James and I would be together. But footballers are special, you know. They have a sort of artistic

ment. And if you're going to be the girlfriend of a
...er star, you have to accept that.

So for a few days I just left him to come to his senses in his
own time, while I drifted along with my own life. Sarah asked
a few probing questions about James at first but I just looked
secretive and said I didn't really want to talk about it, so in the
end she gave up.

Alex didn't, though. Good old Alex! He probably sensed
that I was available again, even though he wasn't to know
that it was temporary. That within a very short time I'd be
back with James again, even closer than before.

Still, in the meantime it was nice to have someone for
company. And Alex was great company, he always had been. So
one night I went for a drink with him after work, and we chatted
away as usual like old friends. I even beat him at darts, although
it's just possible that he let me. After that game, he slaughtered
me three times in a row – just to get his pride back, I suppose.

On the way home we stopped off for some fish and chips.
It was fun being with Alex. I didn't even mind when he said I
had vinegar on my chin, and leaned over to wipe it off with
his tie. A few months before, I'd have been incredibly
embarrassed about that – probably too embarrassed ever to
show my face in public again. Now I just thought it was
funny, and responded by coating a chip in brown sauce and
smearing it all over his face.

"No one does that and gets away with it," he warned me. "You're just going to have to kiss my mouth clean, young woman."

So I did. What was the harm, after all? We were really good friends, and it was so comfortable being with Alex. I could actually press my lips against his without feeling that rocketing dazzle of desire and emotion that shot through me whenever I was anywhere near James. I mean, I couldn't even touch James's hands without feeling as though I'd been juddered with jolts of electricity.

"Hey, enough!" Alex protested. "I'm sure it's all gone by now. No more kissing or I might not behave myself."

I grinned at him, suddenly feeling confident, secure, flirty – all the things I never thought I'd ever be. "Don't you threaten me," I said defiantly, "or you may find you've just stepped over the line."

"I wish!" he answered fervently. "Come on, it's getting all steamy in here. Or is it me? I'll walk you home."

I didn't invite him in or anything and he didn't seem to expect it. He gave me a very gentle kiss, nothing suggestive or sexy.

"Nice to have you back, Katie," he said a little sadly. "How about going to the match on Saturday? Dudlace are at home . . ."

I probably shouldn't have, but I did. I went along with

the rest of the gang were there. It was good to see
y again. She hugged me and said she'd missed me the last
couple of weeks. The others were friendly, too – which was
just as well, I can tell you. Because I wasn't quite prepared for
the impact it would have on me, seeing James running out on
to the pitch, his gorgeous, muscly legs straining in the wind.
Those legs that had so recently been entwined in mine . . .

James played as magically as ever, and soon I was carried
away with the rest of them, shouting and cheering and getting
really worked up when one of the wingers was too slow with
a crucial tactical pass and the other side took dominance over
the ball.

I was pretty quiet after the match though, and decided not
to spend the evening with the others, even though I was
tempted. It was just too intense, being so close to James and
yet so far away. So I went home and spent the evening
watching a nice romantic film and dreaming of how
wonderful it would be when we were back together again . . .

By Monday, I was beginning to get restless. James needed a
reminder, I decided. And a little plan formed in my head. At
lunchtime, I slipped out to the supermarket and blew half my
pay packet on some really expensive ingredients for a
wonderful meal, wine included.

That evening, I rushed home and began to chop vegetables
and fry chicken pieces so that, by the time James's radio show

began, I had a delicious casserole in the oven, and I'd packed everything else – the deliciously thin slivers of Parma ham, the exotic salad with garlic dressing, the lemon tart for dessert.

Tears pricked my eyes as I listened to that velvety voice caressing the airwaves. James, my James! Somehow he seemed to be calling out to me and I knew I just had to respond.

About ten minutes before the show was over, I ordered a cab, loaded the food into it and directed it to James's flat. I'd timed it brilliantly. As we turned the corner, I saw the light from his window, which meant he was back already. He'd told me he usually went straight home, exhausted, after broadcasting.

He'd also said he never had time to eat before the show and was always so hungry afterwards that he would just grab whatever he could find in the fridge, usually ending up with a Marmite sandwich and three or four packets of crisps.

Well, tonight would be different, I told myself excitedly. Tonight would be a feast and a half . . .

He looked surprised when he answered the door. I can't pretend he seemed exactly thrilled, but that didn't bother me. After all, I had promised to give him space and here I was on his doorstep and everything. But he'd soon forgive me, soon see yet another reason why we were just meant for each other.

"Hello," I beamed. "Don't worry, I haven't come to pester

57

you or anything. I just remembered how you never eat properly after your show, and I thought I'd give you a nice surprise."

I didn't give him a chance to object, merely swept past him and into the kitchen, where I busied myself putting the finishing touches to the meal; I popped the casserole into his oven to warm, put the wine in the fridge, laid the table for two and put out the ham in a pretty pattern, decorated with melon slices. I even found some candlesticks and lit a couple of candles.

At first I was rushing around in such a whirl that I didn't look around to see where James was. Now, though, I realized he'd left me to it. He must be in the living-room, waiting for the banquet to be served up.

"You OK?" I called.

"Mmm," he replied from the living-room. "Be with you in a while. I'm . . . er . . . just catching up on the news."

"I'll call you when it's ready, shall I?" I asked. He mumbled agreement. And that was when I had my even better idea. James might be hungry for a good, hot dinner. But somehow I knew he was even hungrier for something else good and hot: me. Of course he was desperate for me, and that must be what he was waiting for.

So I slipped into his bedroom, discarded my clothes and wriggled between the sheets. And that was when I called out to him: "Are you hungry . . . ?" And then added, in my most seductive voice: "Darling, are you starved?"

Then he did appear in the doorway, looking just as sexy and powerful and totally lovable as ever – except for one thing. His face wasn't smiling. His eyes were narrowed, but not with desire. It was more like anger – anger and despair.

"Katie, what are you doing?" he asked wearily.

"I'm here, waiting for you," I faltered, wondering what was going wrong.

With a sigh, he came over to the bed and sat down. He didn't touch me, didn't even look at me. Mostly, he just looked down at his hands, clenched between his knees. His jaw was tense, the muscles all taut round his cheeks. I wanted to stroke him, to kiss away all that anguish and conflict.

"Look, it was sweet of you to make me a meal and everything, Katie, but you shouldn't have done it. Don't you understand?"

"Understand what?" I asked innocently, smiling adoringly at him.

"It's over," he said between gritted teeth. "I thought we'd agreed—"

"Oh, that!" I answered, relieved. "Well, of course we agreed to a little break. I know that. You needed your space and everything. But, well, it's been a week, James. I thought maybe it was enough."

"No, Katie, you've got to listen," James insisted, talking very slowly. "It's over. Really over. I don't want to go out with you any more. In fact, I don't think we ever were going out really. We had one great date and then all of a sudden—"

"Yes, I know," I nodded happily. "All of a sudden we were careering into this wonderful, scary love affair. I'm not surprised you backed off. It was all so fast, wasn't it? But it'll be OK, believe me, James."

"No!" he said forcefully. "No, stop this! I want you to leave, now!"

"OK, OK," I said, upset that he wasn't going to climb into bed and make passionate love to me, but fairly sure that he was really desperate to. He was forcing himself to say no. "I'm going! Look, I'm going! You need more space, I can see that. Enjoy the meal."

He watched in silence as I scrambled into my clothes and made for the door.

"Let me know when you're ready," I said as I left.

"Katie, it's over," he repeated helplessly. "I'm not going to be ready. I want out."

"I'll be waiting!" I assured him.

"There's no point," he argued, shouting through the front door as I made my way down the stairs. "I won't be calling."

"Yes you will!" I called back cheerfully. "You know you will. And take your time, if you need to. I'll always be there for you."

The door slammed, my words no doubt ringing through the keyhole. My plan hadn't gone quite as well as I'd hoped, I realized that. But that night, as I got ready for bed, I had no real doubts that everything would be fine in the end. James loved me, I knew he did. And I loved him.

It wasn't until I was about to have a shower that I realized I wasn't wearing any knickers. I'd definitely had some on when I'd set out. I'd deliberately worn my sexiest pair, transparent black silk ones. So where were they?

While I was brushing my teeth, I thought back over the sequence of events of the evening. I seemed to recall those hot black satin briefs crumpling somewhere under the bed. It was comforting to think of them there, underneath James, watching over him while he slept. Filled with dreamy thoughts of how fantastic it was going to be between us, I drifted off into a deep, romantic sleep.

Seven

"You score every time with me!" That was the message printed round the neck of the cute little cuddly bear, dressed in a football strip, on the front of the card. Inside was scrawled: "I'm there for you always."

I was pleased with that. It was simple but affectionate, fun but with that special hint of passion. Lovingly I licked the envelope, then the stamp. I even sprinkled on just a drop or two of my favourite perfume, Chanel No. 5. It would drive James wild, I thought as I dropped the card into the postbox, I just knew it would!

It'd been a couple of days since our last meeting – the chicken and bed evening, as I liked to call it. I hadn't really expected James to get in touch yet. This was going to be a waiting game and I knew it. But it wouldn't do any harm to send him the odd little reminder occasionally. After all, while

I was convinced we were made for each other, it might take him a little longer to accept the inevitable.

Dreamily, I made my way back to the office and buried myself in work for the whole afternoon. The next day, though, I was back at the shop in the High Street where I'd bought the card. I'd noticed that it came in the same range as an adorable furry toy bear, also dressed in a red and white football strip. He even wore little boots and stripy socks.

I'd resisted him the day before, but I just couldn't get him out of my mind. So today I went in and bought the bear, thinking how sweet he'd look on my mantelpiece. But by the time I got home that evening I'd got a better idea. I wrapped up the bear in red and silver paper and attached a little card which just said: *Hug me until you're back with Katie.*

I had planned to send it through the post the next day, but then I had a better idea. I'd deliver it to the radio station. Then, when James came in to do his show the following Monday, the present would be there, waiting to cheer him up.

'Wake up, Katie!'

Alex was drumming his fingers impatiently on my desk, and I gave a guilty start. I'd been staring into an empty computer screen, deep in thought. I'd no idea how long he'd been standing at my desk, brandishing a pile of new properties to be fed into the general list.

"Sorry – just trying to remember something," I said, putting on a bright smile.

Alex looked concerned. "You OK, Katie?" he asked. "You don't seem quite yourself at the moment."

Well, the last thing I wanted was for Alex – or anyone else – to think there was anything wrong. I mean, just because James and I weren't seeing each other at the moment it didn't mean we weren't together. I knew we were, deep down. So I had every reason to be happy, hadn't I?

So I grinned cheerfully at Alex and answered: "Well, of course I'm not myself after last night. What a disgraceful performance – against a pathetic little southern team, too!"

Alex relaxed, always happy to talk about his favourite subject.

"I'd hardly describe Chelsea as pathetic, Katie, but I do agree we could have mounted a more convincing defence."

"Especially over that offside ruling," I added eagerly. "I mean, I've known schoolboys who wouldn't stoop to that kind of ugly tactic!"

"Oh, really?" replied Alex teasingly. "I didn't think you went in for schoolboys. Not to your taste at all."

'Wrong," I bantered. "I love them, especially on toast with cheese."

Alex's eyes softened, as they occasionally did when we were chatting and joking away like this.

"How about coming with me to the Dudlace match on Saturday?" he suggested. "The others aren't coming, so it'd be just you and me."

I blushed as he spoke, so maybe he thought I was responding to the idea of a cosy little date just with him. In fact, though, I'd gone bright red with excitement at the idea of seeing James again – even at a distance. I remembered how I'd felt last week, how my knees had turned to jelly when he came racing out on to the pitch and how I'd been so overcome with emotion I'd nearly fainted.

"That'd be great," I answered faintly, and tried not to notice how pleased Alex looked, how light his step was as he made his way back to his cluttered desk, whistling the theme tune to *Gavin and Stacey*.

"How about trying a different pub tonight?" I suggested casually. "Let's try that one we went to after we'd helped out with the football phone-in. What was it called . . ."

"The Chariot of Fire," offered Alex, giving me a long stare.

"That's the one," I said, snapping my fingers as though I'd forgotten – as though the name of the pub, its every table, every patch of stained wallpaper, every football trophy ranged on the shelves, wasn't carved on my heart.

Oh, I knew the Chariot of Fire all right. It was a landmark in our love affair, James's and mine. And landmarks are there to be revisited.

It was early evening after the match on Saturday. I'd managed to keep my feelings pretty well under control, even though I'll admit my heart was racing at the very sight of James. When he scored a goal I think I must have screeched like a parrot, even more loudly than the rest of the supporters. And that's saying something!

But by then I had my little secret to keep me going. That very morning I'd gone down to Radio Dudlace and asked if I could leave something for James Angel. The girl on Reception looked a bit weary, as if people were always wanting to leave messages for him. But I explained this was special, I was his girlfriend.

She was about to take the parcel and put it into James's pigeon hole, clearly labelled on the wall behind her, when a frantic voice boomed out through the tannoy: "Francesca! Francesca! Help! The computer's crashed again and there's only three more minutes to go before the next jingle."

It was a voice I knew well: the local DJ Adam Boxer, who did a really popular request show on Saturday mornings. Francesca leapt to attention and went rushing off to the studio to rescue him.

Which was handy for me. I slipped round the desk, and as

I popped the bear into James's pigeon hole I couldn't help noticing something else nestling there. I reached out, unable to help myself. It was a Filofax. James must have left it somewhere, and he'd be so pleased to get it back!

Almost without thinking about it, I slipped it into my handbag. If James was going to be grateful to someone, I told myself, it might as well be me.

When I got back home, I flicked through it until I came to contacts. My name wasn't there, but that was hardly surprising. You don't need to store the personal details of the woman you love, not when they're carved on your heart.

Just for interest, though, I checked the diary entry. Today's match was in, then for the evening, he'd just put "*Chariot. FP*." I thought quickly. That must mean a football party at the Chariot of Fire. Well, maybe he was going to have a surprise guest or two!

At the bottom of the page I wrote: *I will always love you. Yours for ever, Katie.*

Then I put the Filofax in my bag and got ready for the match.

Although it was late March and the sun was shining brightly, it was still cold and windy and I was glad of my thick jacket. But even then, I was shivering a bit as Alex and I left the grounds slightly disconsolate at the disappointing 2–2 draw against Sunfield.

Alex put his arm round me in a friendly kind of way. "Cold?" he asked solicitously.

"A bit," I admitted. "How about coming back to my place for some nice hot crumpets with honey?"

"You wicked, wicked woman!" Alex said happily. "How did you know there's nothing I like more than—"

"Don't say it!" I shouted, laughing.

"Than a nice bit of crumpet," he added, despite my protests.

We were still laughing when we got home. I put the kettle on while he settled down in my neat, cosy little living-room.

"Nice," he commented as I brought in the tea. "It's like you, this place: pretty, compact, organized . . ."

"Ugh! You make me sound like an office," I said, and we both laughed again.

It was really easy being with Alex. He had a wonderful way of making himself at home, sprawling out on the floor to look at my very small collection of CDs as he munched on his fourth crumpet.

"Great! *The Cure*," he said approvingly, and put it on, selecting his favourite track as if he actually lived there.

We sat side by side and listened to the music companionably. It was nice having Alex there, I acknowledged to myself. He wasn't James, of course. Naturally there was nothing like that about it. But it felt so comfortable being with him that I didn't protest when he moved closer towards me, circled his arm round my shoulders and gently kissed me.

It felt good, it really did. His mouth was firm on mine, but his lips were soft and sweet. For a while we remained locked together, then slid apart. I squeezed his hand to show it was OK, that I was glad about the kiss but not to read too much into it. At least, I hoped that was what it showed.

He looked puzzled, then brightly suggested we go for a drink. And that was when I said I'd like to try somewhere a bit different – and he fell right into my trap.

The Chariot of Fire was buzzing with Saturday night frenzy by the time we arrived. I managed to grab a table and while Alex went to get the drinks I did a hasty survey of the whole room. I recognized a few of the regulars who'd been there the last time I'd been in with James. There were two of his mates, there was another guy from the team. And there was James himself, lording it as usual in the centre of a vast crowd of admirers. There was that blonde, pretty girl with the spiky hair, obviously trying her hardest to get near him.

I noticed she was on orange juice again. Her hair was even spikier than before and she wore a skin-tight leopard print top. There was a bloke sitting next to her who was probably her boyfriend, but I didn't really blame her for being more interested in James. The other bloke was so ordinary compared with him.

Alex arrived at the table balancing our drinks plus two packets of crisps and mixed nuts. I decided to ignore the James party for a while – playing hard to get, I think it's called. So I concentrated on talking to Alex for a while, until he suggested that we go on for a pizza.

As we left the heaving, crowded pub, I told Alex to wait for me outside, then squeezed my way right up to where James was sitting. He looked startled to see me, but I wasn't put off.

"Hello, stranger!" I said with the sweetest smile.

"Er . . . hi!" he said, staring at me as if he'd seen a ghost.

"Don't worry, I'm not staying," I assured him. "I just wanted to give you this." And I handed him the organizer.

"Thanks – but . . . erm . . . where did you get it?"

I beamed at him. "Do you know, it's the most amazing thing. I found it at the grounds, just this afternoon, when I was queuing up for the ladies at half-time. There it was, half-hidden under the steps."

James looked suitably astonished, almost disbelieving. Then he shrugged.

"Well, thanks again. It was nice of you to return it. Erm . . . see you around, Katie."

"Yes, OK – see you!" I answered as cheerfully as I could, then waved as I disappeared back into the crowds.

It was so hard to leave him, so very hard to appear cool and bouncy when inside I was eaten up with turmoil, longing to touch him, hold him, for the two of us to be caught up once again in a wild embrace.

So even though I was quite sure he was going to come back to me in the end, I was a little subdued when I rejoined Alex outside the pub. Still, it was good to have someone there for me and I soon cheered up when we got to the restaurant. We shared a Neapolitana pizza plus a huge helping of chocolate fudge cake with ice-cream and then, feeling full and much happier, we linked arms and tried to dance all the way home. I think we were aiming for a kind of Dizzee Rascal, but ended up more like Dorothy and the Lion in *The Wizard of Oz*.

Alex kissed me again when we got to my door. And again it was good – very sweet. I didn't invite him in and I don't think he expected me to. After all, it wasn't as if he was my boyfriend. We worked in the same office, that was all. And that was a good enough reason for keeping things cool. So we had that one long, lingering kiss – and then said goodnight.

Eight

I don't want you to get the idea I was completely deluded all this time. I mean, I might have been in love but I wasn't stupid. Sure, I had my doubts sometimes. There was that nagging little voice of reason, deep down, that kept intruding on my dreams and telling me to forget about James – it was over. But I so desperately wanted to believe he felt the same way about me that I felt about him, that I did everything I could to ignore it. You could say that I chose not to face reality.

The one person who seemed to understand what was happening to me was Holly. And she was such a good friend to me at that time that I very nearly lost her. That's what happens when you don't want to hear the truth.

She rang me at work a few days after the chance meeting with James that I'd engineered so cleverly. I hadn't seen her for a while so I was pleased to hear from her, especially when she said she'd missed me. We met for lunch that day, and it wasn't long before she was firing questions at me, all about James.

I told her far more than I'd intended. Holly was like that: she could get things out of you just by being a good listener. Soon I'd confided in her about that disastrous night when I'd brought round a meal for him, and all about the little messages I sent him, and the bear.

She looked horrified, her eyes wide in disbelief.

"No!" she kept exclaiming. "You didn't! Then what? Oh, no – you didn't?"

I couldn't help laughing, her dismay was so obvious.

"What's the matter, Holly? I'm only doing it for his own good. Eventually he'll realize I was right all along. We belong together, we really do."

Holly gave me a long, sympathetic stare. She was probably thinking that I didn't look the part of James's girlfriend, and she had a point. I didn't bother with my appearance so much now, knowing that I wasn't going to be seeing him. I was wearing a frumpy black cardigan over a floppy T-shirt and jeans and my hair needed washing.

"I know what you're thinking," I said. "I look a bit of a mess today, don't I? Obviously James likes me to dress up for him, and I do. But looks aren't that important to him. It's the real me he's interested in."

Again, Holly just looked at me as if she wanted to say something. Then she thought better of it, and suggested we go shopping later in the week. And we had such a good time then that we agreed to meet for coffee the following Saturday morning.

It was clear from the moment we'd ordered our cappuccinos and chocolate muffins that Holly had something to say to me, and she was plucking up all her courage to say it.

"Seen James at all?" she asked casually.

I shrugged. "No, I told you – we're not seeing each other at the moment. But I know we'll be back together soon. Just you wait."

Holly sighed and began to spoon froth into her mouth thoughtfully.

"Yeah, sure," she said at last. "But while you're not actually seeing James, what are you doing about Alex?"

I felt a blush spreading round my cheeks. Holly's boyfriend Sam was Alex's best friend. One of them must have put her up to this.

"What do you mean?" I hedged.

"Katie, he really likes you," Holly told me earnestly.

"Yes, well, I like him too," I answered sheepishly.

"You know what I mean," Holly retorted. "He wants to go out with you and he just doesn't know what's going on. You keep playing hot and cold with him. What's he supposed to think?"

"I don't know what you mean," I protested. "Alex knows I'm going out with James. He and I are just friends."

"Oh, do stop this, Katie!" Holly burst out, infuriated. "You're not going out with James. Even you know you're not. You may think you're going to get back together but you're the only one who does. He's not interested in you, Katie. Can't you see that? He was just using you—"

"How dare you say that!" I flashed back, incensed but fearful too. That little nagging voice inside me was getting louder, telling me that Holly was right. "James loves me; I know he does. How could I expect you to understand?"

"Of course he doesn't love you," Holly shouted back. "If he loved you he'd be there with you, not down the pub going through every girl on the Dudlace fan club mailing list."

"That's not true!" I wailed. "Why are you saying these things?"

"I'm saying them to make you see sense," retorted Holly. "Look, there's this guy who never rings you, never sees you, doesn't want anything to do with you – and you think he's madly in love with you! I don't get it. I really don't. But I want to help you see sense and get over it."

"Well, thanks but no thanks," I told her, trembling with anger and anxiety. "Why don't you just find another hopeless case to waste your pity on? I don't need it, especially from you. I mean, isn't it enough that you nag poor old Sam, without getting started on me, too? You should start concentrating a bit more, you know, Holly. All you ever do is criticize him. No wonder he's starting to look elsewhere for a little bit of comfort and joy."

As I stormed out I caught a glimpse of Holly's face, crumpled and hurt, shattered by the spite of my words. And I was sorry. I hadn't meant any of it; I'd just wanted to get back at her for what she'd said to me. Of course they weren't true. I knew that. But it was too late. I'd said it. And I'd probably lost the only real friend I'd ever had.

I was more unsettled by my conversation with Holly than I wanted to admit, even to myself. The terrible problem was, she was voicing exactly the same doubts that were plaguing me, the very ones I didn't want to hear. Suppose she was right? I asked myself tormentedly. Suppose I really was fooling myself, and James really didn't have any feelings for me? Worst of all, what if Holly was right about those other women? I simply couldn't bear the thought of him being with anyone else.

Then two things happened to distract me – indeed, to banish all my troubled thoughts. The first was that soon after I got back home after meeting Holly, the doorbell rang. I rushed down to answer it, noticing that there were some letters on the mat that must have arrived while I was out. I picked them up, then answered the door.

There, looking anxious and eager, stood Alex. His hands were covered in oil, and it was smeared on his face and his tatty jeans. He didn't look his best.

"Er . . . hi!" he began nervously. "I was just passing this way when I got a puncture and, well, you know me, very handy with a jack and a wrench, I thought I'd change the wheel in a jiffy. But I didn't have the right-sized jiffy, so it took a bit longer than I'd . . . erm . . . hoped . . ."

I laughed. Alex was very appealing when he talked his mad nonsense. Even if he was covered in oil.

"So you've managed to change the wheel all by yourself," I said, encouragingly.

"Eventually, yes," he answered. Then he added shyly, "But I got a bit messy and since I was nearby I thought maybe you wouldn't mind if I came in to wash my hands."

I opened the door wider and let him through. As he climbed the stairs to the bedsit, I asked: "Just exactly where did this puncture happen, Alex?"

"Oh, very near here," he said. Then he mentioned the road, which was a good ten-minute walk away. I couldn't help laughing again.

"What a coincidence, you breaking down right outside my door," I commented, feeling flattered at his obvious ploy.

"Well, you know, it was a bit of an excuse really," he admitted. "I just wanted the chance to sample your fabulous luxury soap and matching bath foam. And . . . er . . . and also to see if you might be free to come out with me tonight."

As he locked himself in the bathroom, accompanied by the sounds of gushing water and tuneless singing, I thought guiltily of Holly's warning that Alex really liked me. Then I shrugged. What was wrong with going out with him? He knew the score, didn't he? He knew I was really with someone else.

Idly I flicked through the envelopes in my hand. There was a telephone bill, a printed circular telling me I was going to be entered in a prize draw, a flyer from the local dry cleaners, and two more interesting looking personal letters.

The first was addressed in capital letters, on a bright green envelope. Inside was a lurid postcard, a reproduction of the billboard advertising one of those terrible old-fashioned B-movies called *Wasp Woman*. The picture was of a swarm of wasps with this evil-looking woman leading them towards a terrified, cowering man. Clipped to it was an anonymous message. It simply said: *Careful you don't end up like this. Buzz, buzz, buzz!*

I went pale, horrified that anyone could hate me enough to send me such a spiteful message. I took another look at the envelope and breathed a sigh of relief. It just said: "To whom it may concern." They must have picked the wrong door, I told myself. But it was still unnerving to have opened such a malevolent, crazy note.

The other envelope was blue and definitely addressed to me. I ripped it open excitedly, sure that it must contain a card. And it did. On the front was a picture of the Dudlace football ground. I'd seen cards like it every time I'd been to a match. My heart began to pound. It had to be, it must be – it was from James.

I read it with bated breath. Then, incredulous, I read it again. He couldn't mean it surely?

Dear Katie,
I've tried to ignore your messages and presents but this
time you've gone too far. I don't know how you got hold
of my organizer but you had no right to use it. Please
leave me alone.
James

Transfixed, I stared at the cruel, clipped message. He couldn't mean it, I told myself desperately, he just couldn't! There had to be some mistake. Maybe he was so confused about his feelings that he just couldn't take it. Or maybe he hadn't even written the note himself. It could have been the team manager, who hated the players to get distracted from the game. One of his mates could have sent it for a joke, or perhaps – yes, this seemed the most likely – perhaps some girl who fancied him had seen my message in the Filofax and decided to warn me off. The more I thought about it, the more I tried to convince myself that James hadn't sent the note at all.

The little nagging voice was there, of course, telling me not to be so stupid, to face up to it and admit that James didn't want me, didn't even want to hear from me. Either way, I told myself, I just had to find out. And there was only one way I could think of to do that.

At that moment Alex emerged from the bathroom, looking slightly cleaner, but still very scruffy. I couldn't help comparing his lanky hair and torn clothes with James's lithe elegance.

"Wow! Thanks, Katie," he grinned. "Good job I was so near your place. Shall I make some coffee?"

I shrugged, far too preoccupied to think about such mundane matters.

"Are you going to the Dudlace match this afternoon?" I asked casually.

"Nope," Alex said regretfully. "For once, I'm having to give it a miss. I've got to help my sister move flat. That's why I had to repair my car. Myself. You did take in, didn't you, that I actually changed that wheel all by myself?"

"Yes, and I think you should get a medal," I told him,

forcing myself to smile, "or at least a formal email. I'll do you one right away."

While he made coffee I sat at my computer and created an exact replica of the office email. I addressed it from me, with copies to all colleagues. It read:

Congratulations on the successful accomplishment of your personal objective of changing the wheel on your car. The company would like to take this opportunity to thank you for all your efforts over the past weeks, and to recommend you for promotion to full macho man.

"Hey, this is great," Alex enthused, when I handed a print-out of the email to him. "Does this mean you will go out with me tonight?"

There was a pleading look in his eyes that made me feel really uncomfortable. So I just looked away before answering. "Yes, I'd like that, Alex. You're a really good friend, you know?"

"I know," he said sadly. "Pick you up at eight, then. In my brilliantly repaired car."

Nine

It was a relief, to be honest, when Alex said he couldn't go to the match. I'd operate far more efficiently on my own. So that afternoon I took myself off, bought my ticket and sat in the stands alone, cheering when Dudlace did well and thrilling inside whenever I caught a glimpse of James – my James. Even just seeing his brilliantly honed body, his amazing feet that performed such magic whenever he was near the ball, made me feel warm inside. Of course it was me he wanted! Of course we were made for each other!

Some of my euphoria evaporated as the game neared to a close – and it wasn't just because we were losing badly to a very mediocre team whose form that season had been laughable up until now. That was just depressing. But as I slipped out of my seat and made my way to the players' entrance, to take my place among the twelve-year-old autograph hunters and the usual gaggle of groupie hopefuls, I was feeling more than just depressed. I was quaking with nerves, terrified of what I might discover.

And I was right, too. I had every reason to be fearful. As the minutes crept painfully by, I became more and more anxious. What was taking them so long? Surely, after that ignominious 4–1 defeat, all they'd want to do was slink away?

At last they began to emerge, and the little crowd around me began to swarm round them proffering their autograph books, firing questions at them, flirting, chatting . . .

Then I saw him. James was looking understandably fed-up after that unbelievably poor performance, but he was still stunningly good-looking. I wanted to smooth away the furrows from his brow, bring a smile back to those ravaged features. It had to be OK, I told myself desperately. It just had to.

"James!" I called out, smiling with pleasure as if this was a chance meeting with an old friend. He looked up, as if he couldn't quite believe what he'd just heard. His face was – well, it's still painful to remember this, but all I can say is his face was a mask of horror. He looked as if he'd seen a poltergeist.

"Didn't you get my letter?" he asked, his voice so icy that several people turned to stare at me.

"Oh, of course I got it," I floundered, my heart sinking.

"But I thought probably you felt you had to write it. I knew you didn't mean it . . ."

As I blathered on, barely aware of what I was saying, only trying to keep up some form of communication with him, I was suddenly aware that my elbows were being grasped by strong, practised hands. Two men, soberly dressed, unobtrusive but exceptionally firm, were leading me away. I was still calling after James, still trying to convince him that it was me he needed, me he truly loved, while they manoeuvred me into the street and away from the man who'd turned my life upside-down and then left me to hang.

By the time Alex picked me up that evening I'd recovered – outwardly, at any rate. I'd made a bit of an effort to hide the swirling emotions, the hurt and humiliation that threatened to engulf me. I was wearing one of the new skin-tight tops that were just beginning to feel part of me after all those years of frumpy clothes. This one was black, and looked great with my tight trousers and knee-high boots. I'd even found time to put on some purple sparkly nail varnish and matching eyeshadow.

No one was going to know how broken up I was inside, especially not Alex. I decided I owed it to him to give him a chance. He didn't have James's film star looks, his brilliance, his perfect sinewy body, his fame and charisma, but at least he wanted to be with me, and that was important. I was only just beginning to realize how much.

He arrived on the dot of eight, dressed as usual in one of his shapeless jumpers, with a crumpled blue shirt peeping over the neck. He'd changed his jeans into some cleaner ones, but that was about it. With a stinging pain in my heart I remembered again James's crisp good looks, his shining white shirts and that easy, casual elegance. How could I force myself to forget him – to feel that way about someone else?

But I did my best. I smiled a warm welcome, and was gratified when Alex let out a low whistle of appreciation.

"You look great, Katie – gorgeous!" he told me. And then he spoilt it by adding: "You know, it's hard to believe that you were ever that timid, mousy little thing that turned up at the office three months ago, too frightened to ask where the toilet was."

I grinned good-humouredly, but only to hide how bleak that made me feel. The trouble was, Alex was right. I'd spent my whole life being shy and frumpy, and that's what I still was, underneath. A few coats of nail varnish and a slinky top can't really change the way you are, can they?

I tried to tell myself not to be so soft. I'd come a long way in two months. I'd made friends, found a new style, developed a bit of confidence – and been swept off my feet by the most wonderful man in the world.

But it was no good. I couldn't ignore that nagging voice in my head, the one that was always ready with the hard, hurtful truth. *You've been dumped by the most wonderful man in the world because you're nothing but a boring frump,* insisted the voice, no matter now desperately I tried to silence it.

Torn between that awful sense of desperation and my new-found confidence, I went ahead and tried to enjoy my evening with Alex. We went to the cinema and had a good laugh at the latest Will Ferrell film, sharing a huge tub of popcorn and even vaster cartons of Coke. Afterwards, he drove me home. When he pulled up outside my place, while the engine was still running, he turned and gave me a quizzical look.

"I'm hungry," he said at last. "I knew we should have gone out to eat."

"I'll make us some pasta," I suggested. Only then did he turn off the engine. Alex was taking it slowly and so was I.

But I had to admit that it felt good being with him. He was so easy to talk to – it was really relaxing after the rollercoaster of emotions I'd suffered lately, or the intense, tight excitement of those few precious times with James.

While I prepared the food, Alex told me about his sister, who'd just moved into her own flat in town. He'd been helping her all afternoon. He lived in a house with Sam and a couple of other guys.

"You must come for a meal, Katie," he said eagerly. "It's not – well, I don't think you'll find it very tidy. We're not houseproud."

"What a surprise!" I laughed. "I'm not that easy to shock, you know. I don't expect the whole world to clean behind the fridge every day, or keep their dvds in alphabetical order."

"You do that?" he exclaimed, pretending to be horrified.

"Well, yes, I happen to like systems," I defended myself. "But I realize not everyone's like that. Just as long as you don't keep baked beans in the tin once they're opened, or put dead matches back in the box with the new ones, or leave your sheets on for more than a month."

"That's your ultimate test in cleanliness, is it?" Alex asked doubtfully.

"Yes, I think that just about covers it." I mused. "Oh, and dishes left in the sink for more than a day."

"Oh, no!" Alex clapped his hand to his head. "I was just breathing a sigh of relief over my pass rate and now I've failed over a few dishes. What a shame!"

Just before I served up the meal, Alex disappeared and returned with a bottle of wine. We clinked glasses and began to eat, companionably quiet except for his occasional exclamations about the food.

"It's only pasta and salad," I protested, laughing. "Nothing special."

"Must be the company then," Alex said, and he must have noticed how I froze at his intimate tone, the meaning in his voice. He reached over and took my hand in his.

"Don't shy away from me, Katie," he said softly. "It's not a crime to let someone get close to you, you know."

Then he leaned across the table and pressed his lips very gently on mine. I closed my eyes, wishing it was James talking to me so tenderly, kissing me with such gentleness. But the feeling just wasn't there.

Alex led me away from the table and pulled me down next to him on the sofa.

"Katie, listen. I know you've been hurt." I opened my mouth to protest, but he took no notice. "You don't have to talk about it. You don't need to say anything. I'm not trying to rush you into anything, you know. I just like you and I want to get to know you a little better."

And then he was kissing me again. There were no electric sparks, no rush of passion, no wild abandon. But oh, it was so good to be wanted! To be treated kindly. I let that kiss go on and on, my hands creeping round his neck and pulling him closer towards me, never wanting to let him go.

In the end it was Alex who pulled away. He looked at me for a few moments, then smiled.

"Nice," he said. This was quite a disappointment, really. I'd expected him to be ecstatic. Instead he just said: "So let's take it slowly. No commitments, no expectations. But I'd like to go out with you again some time. How about it?"

I nodded. He kissed me again, then got up and said goodnight. And even though my heart was still with James, I couldn't help feeling bereft as the door closed behind him. In fact, I thought I'd never, ever felt so utterly alone.

Just as I thought my weekend couldn't get any worse, I found another, brilliant way to make myself utterly wretched: I went home to see my parents for Sunday lunch.

This turned out to be a big mistake. Other girls could run home to their mum and dad to be cuddled and taken care of. Other girls would know that whatever they thought of themselves there was one person who thought they were beautiful and perfect: their dad. And one person who could magic away all their troubles and pain: their mum.

Well, it just wasn't like that in my family, and even though I'd been away from them for three whole months, it didn't seem to make any difference. Even though my mum had actually rung me to invite me over, which meant deep down she must want to see me, I knew from the moment she opened the front door that nothing had changed.

She looked me up and down, her face set into her habitual sour, rather disappointed scowl. I'd considered flinging my arms around her neck, just to show her I cared, but we weren't a very huggy sort of family, and it wasn't as though she was exactly welcoming.

"What do you think you look like?" she greeted me.

I flinched. I'd thought really hard about what I was going to wear, decided against my favourite black jeans, and instead put on a black miniskirt dotted with a print of bright flowers, a tight red top and a black satin jacket. And a pair of red Converses to match.

"Don't you like it?" I asked, deflated, as I made my way through the dingy hallway into the living-room where my dad was watching Sky Sport.

"Look at the way she's got herself out," Mum said to him.

He glanced my way, nodded and said: "Hello, love – about time you paid us a visit. Thought you'd forgotten all about us."

Then he went back to the racing, and I wandered into the kitchen, feeling completely useless as I always did when my mum was preparing a meal. She wasn't a great cook but she was very organized and didn't allow anything to get in the way of her routine. So she brushed me aside impatiently when I offered to shell the peas, and tutted to herself when I asked if I could do anything else to help.

"Ridiculous," she muttered, "getting yourself out in those silly clothes! I've never held with cheap fashion. And as for your skirt . . ."

"It's not that short," I said defensively. "Everyone wears them. There's a girl at work who wears hers at least five centimetres shorter than this."

"Disgusting!" Mum sniffed. "Showing off everything – your legs, everything. It's not how you were brought up, my girl. And don't think you look nice, all skinny like that. You just look haggard. You haven't the build for it, you see. Big bones. You were born plump and plump is what you should have stayed."

I sighed, wanting to shout out that she couldn't treat me like this, not now. I was a grown-up, living by myself, sorting out my own life. But that wasn't how it felt inside. It was like being twelve years old all over again, shrinking into a little ball of pain at my mother's constant nagging, her criticism, her conviction that I was ugly and stupid and pointless.

The only nice thing about the whole ordeal was that there was an extra guest for lunch – my Great Aunt Judy. It turned out she'd specially asked Mum to invite me along because she wanted to see me. She lived in a little village not far from Dudlace, but this weekend she was visiting Mum and Dad before going off on one of her journeys.

Great Aunt Judy was my mother's aunt, but completely different from her in every way. She was good fun, for one thing, with a rich deep giggle and twinkly eyes. And while my mother shuddered at anything new or different, hated anything that got in the way of her routine, Judy loved adventures. She was always rushing off to take up pottery classes or flying lessons, and at least once a year she'd go on an exotic holiday.

Widowed years ago, Judy lived by herself in a pretty cottage. As a child I'd always envied her. She always seemed excited by life. And for some reason she really liked me, too. I remembered when I was quite little, overhearing her berating my mother about me.

"You really must show her you're on her side," she scolded. "That child is like a candle – the flame flickering because there's not enough oxygen. Without a little encouragement, it just might go out altogether."

"Stuff and nonsense!" my mum had replied briskly. "I don't believe in spoiling children and I certainly don't believe in lying to them. Katherine hasn't a great deal going for her, let's face it."

I still cringed, remembering those callous words.

"You'll regret it," Great Aunt Judy had warned her sadly. "Katie is a sweet, loving girl, but I think you're squeezing all the joy out of her."

I'd loved her for that, loved her for thinking I had any worth at all. So I was genuinely delighted when her familiar round form came bustling into the house, her face beaming with pleasure as she gave me a firm, decisive hug.

"Katie, dear! So glad you could come. I wanted to ask you a little favour."

She explained that she was about to embark on a longer trip than usual this time – a really exciting one.

"I'm off to the Middle East to join an archaeological dig in Jordan," she announced. "I had to fib a little bit – said I'd done a lot of digs, named a few famous ones from so long ago no one would be able to check up. Anyhow, I'll be gone for three months, so I was rather hoping you'd be able to keep an eye on the cottage for me."

I didn't get a chance to answer. She swept on telling me about the arrangements she'd made. A neighbour would tend the garden during the summer, another friend was looking after the cats. But she didn't like the idea of leaving the house completely unlived in.

"So if you'd just visit from time to time I'd be most grateful, dear," she said, as though that was all decided. "I know you've got your own place now, but Greenacres is a dear little cottage for weekends, not all that far from Dudlace, really. Well, of course Stoniton is a little out of the way, but you can always get someone to drive you there, can't you? I'd be quite happy for you to put up a few friends."

"Friends!" snorted my mother. "Don't you kid yourself. Katie doesn't have any friends, do you, dear?"

"Well – as a matter of fact, I have made a few—"

"What are they after?" Mum demanded suspiciously. "Not your company, I'll be bound. I suppose it's your friends who've got you to starve yourself to death and put on ridiculous clothes. Some friends!"

Anxious to change the subject, Judy butted in. "How about boyfriends, Katie? Any young man you want to tell us about?" As I blushed deeply and didn't answer, Judy turned to my dad and added: "Well, I think she looks lovely – really pretty. I always said she'd be a beauty, didn't I?"

My mum just glared, my dad nodded absently and cast his gaze back to the television which was now blaring out Formula One.

Somehow I struggled through the day and, with huge relief, escaped home again. I felt bruised and hurt, as I always used to after a gruelling session with my mum. But in my purse was the key to Judy's cottage, and that cheered me up, somehow.

At least it showed someone cared about me. Judy hadn't really needed a house-minder, I was fairly sure. She'd just wanted to offer me a refuge, a place of calm and quiet in the country, where I could be myself. And that mattered more than anything – more than I even realized right then. I'd been battered from all sides that weekend, I reflected, as I snuggled down to bed at last. But at least someone had shown me a little kindness. And that vaguely comforted me, as I cried myself to sleep.

And now it was Monday morning, and once again my world seemed to be shattering round me. I'd gone into my usual routine – making the coffee, collecting the mail, switching on the computer and then checking the telephone voicemail. I always did everything in the same order – that's me all over.

After I'd written down the messages, I clicked on to email with one hand, while ordering the post with the other. And that was when I got my real shock. A message flashed up:

Leave him alone! Leave him alone! Leave him alone!

It was repeated at least a hundred times, filling my entire screen.

It was such a shock I nearly fainted. A red flash blinded my eyes. My heart was pounding so hard I thought I would explode. And my hands were trembling uncontrollably, shaking the sheaf of letters until they scattered to the floor.

"Katie, are you OK?" Alex, dear deluded Alex, was at my side in an instant, his voice full of concern. He must have glanced at me across the office, probably to smile that secret smile he was getting so practised at, and noticed my distress. But I couldn't let him see the cause of it. Of course I couldn't.

So I blinked a couple of times until my eyes were able to focus again, smiled bravely at him, and hurriedly clicked a couple of times on my computer screen. "Yes, I'm fine,"

I managed to say. "I – I felt a bit faint, that's all. Entirely my own fault – for skipping breakfast."

"Stay right there," Alex ordered. "I'll get you a coffee. Oh, and I know just what you need." He raced over to his own desk, burrowed in the mounds of paperwork, sticky tape, used pens and ancient Post-its, and eventually emerged from the mess brandishing a Mars Bar. "Here!" He tossed it over so that it landed in my lap. "Eat it. Right away. I insist."

As I forced myself to chew on the chocolate bar, my mind was racing as I tried to think who could possibly have sent such a vicious, deranged message. First, I tried to check the address it had come from but it was one of those anonymous companies that I'd never be able to trace.

But then I thought about who might know me and where I worked. There weren't many suspects. I still had pitifully few friends. There was only one who fitted the bill. At least, she'd been a friend until very recently. Holly. It had to be Holly. She'd been so angry at what I'd said about Sam, and so adamant that I should stop seeing James.

This was her way of hurting me back, I realized, just as I'd hurt her with my thoughtless, cruel remarks. Then I remembered that other message – the one that came with the Wasp Woman card. That had to be from Holly too, I realized. Of course, she wouldn't have had time to send it. She must have delivered it by hand immediately after our row on Saturday morning.

I was so upset I was still shaking when Alex brought me some coffee. I hated Holly for persecuting me like this, hated myself for hurting her, too. What a mess! What a truly terrible, agonizing mess!

Ten

I went home early that day. I just couldn't concentrate. Four times in a row I'd accessed the wrong property list for Jake; then I furnished Sarah with a detailed breakdown of all to-let sites in the northside area, but for the previous year; and finally, Alex overheard me confidently sending a client to inspect a house that had actually been burned down several weeks ago.

"You're not well," he said, concerned. "This is so unlike you. Why don't you take the rest of the day off?" And everyone else murmured their agreement. I was usually so reliable. You could tell it had unsettled them to see me like this.

But none of them had any idea what they'd sent me back to, the misery that was waiting for me behind my own front door.

It was nothing much, really, I suppose. Not on its own. It

was just that when I opened the door to the flat there, on the mat, was a disgusting, smelly old rag. It was all crumpled up and had obviously been posted through the letter-box.

I recoiled, then stared at it in horror, not really wanting to touch. Tentatively, I bent down and saw that a small sticky label had been attached to one corner. Edging forward, I lifted it with the very tips of two fingers and read two scrawled words: *toe rag*. I shuddered, tears springing to my eyes. It was such a venomous, spiteful act. Someone really must hate me.

As I transported the offensive rag to the dustbin, holding it as far from my nose as possible, I thought about Holly – fun-loving, down-to-earth, sensible Holly, who until recently had been such a friend to me. Could she really have turned against me so viciously? It was hard to imagine. But then, I suppose my own words to her had been harsh and out of character, too.

Feeling sick and miserable, I curled up in bed and tried to sleep, but every fitful doze was interrupted by nasty thoughts intruding into my dreams. After a long while I realized it was nearly dark. I fumbled for the radio and switched it on, hoping for a little company.

And what should I hear but James's voice – his strong, velvety tones caressing me through the airwaves. Of course, it was Monday evening! His show had just begun. I wanted to hide my head under the covers to banish every sound of him but somehow I couldn't. I still loved him so much – even this contact was better than nothing.

Tonight he was trying out a new idea. Listeners had to vote for their favourite football moments and he would play the clips. They'd already had the "Miracle of Istanbul", 2005, when after being down 3–0, Liverpool made a sensational come-back against Milan, winning on penalties.

"Now I really must congratulate this next listener," James was saying. "She's asked me to withhold her name but all I can tell you is, she's a really juicy dish with a plum suggestion. She's asked for John Terry's penalty miss for Chelsea against Manchester United, in the 2008 Champion League finals.

I didn't hear it, wasn't aware of anything except the pounding in my ears, the churning inside me as those few words repeated over and over in my head like a dirge. Who was she, this dish of a girl? Did she exist at all? Was she the reason he'd thrown me over? Surely he wouldn't be so brutal?

Wearily, I turned off the radio and forced myself to the kitchen to make a sandwich. It was over, I told myself. Only a real nutcase would have persisted for this long. James had made it clear he didn't want to see me. He'd even had a couple of heavies escort me away from him. And now, it sounded like there might even be a new girl in his life. It was time to start again, I decided. I'd carry on seeing Alex, try to make it up with Holly, and put James behind me.

I rang Holly but she was out so I left a message on her answerphone. I said I was sorry for the things I'd said about Sam, and I really wanted to be friends again. Then I watched *Casablanca*, had a good cry, and was still crying when I went back to bed and to a night of troubled dreams.

The next day I tripped into work, determined to be just as alert and organized as I possibly could. Alex was waiting for me with a cup of coffee and a bacon sandwich.

"Hey, how are you feeling?" he asked earnestly. "I didn't ring last night because I thought you'd probably want to sleep it off. But just in case you're not looking after yourself, I got you some breakfast."

I laughed. "Actually, I did have some toast, but only a very small piece. I'm starving – which must mean I'm better. Thanks."

I pretended an appetite I really didn't feel, forced myself to wolf down the sandwich, and then charged into my usual routine only twice as fast. Everyone was relieved that I seemed to be myself again, and it certainly helped to be busy. I was deep in a completely new, improved system I'd started to devise when the phone rang. It was Holly.

"Katie? I'm so glad you rang," she gushed. "I'm sorry too – about all the things I said. Let's have lunch really soon. I want to show you these shoes I've fallen in love with."

There was a pause. Holly had said she was sorry about the things she'd said. But what about the things she'd done? "All right," I replied cautiously. "But no more messages, OK?"

"What?" Holly asked, sounding genuinely puzzled.

"Look, there's no need to pretend," I told her quietly. "I don't blame you, honestly. You were angry and I was out of line. I'm willing to forget it if you are. But let's agree to no more of those scare tactics."

"Katie, I truly don't know what you're talking about," Holly told me.

"OK then," I said tersely, "let's refresh your memory, shall we? What did you do straight after our little coffee morning conversation on Saturday?"

"Oh, that, Holly said, obviously relieved. "Oh, I see what you mean. Well, I thought I was doing it for the best. But if it upset you, of course I'm sorry – really sorry. Look, let's meet and sort it all out, shall we? How about Friday?"

Something didn't quite ring true about the conversation, but I was too relieved to worry about it. My life may be falling apart, I thought, happily constructing yet another complicated spreadsheet, but at least I've got a friend out there.

And then things began to look up even more. The flashing on my screen told me I had a new message. It was an email from Alex. I glanced across the room. There he was, deep in conversation with a client. I glanced back to the message:

Really glad you're better. Even more glad you're wearing that stripy top. It brings out the colour of your eyes. I can't risk looking at you today or I won't get any work done at all. So how about coming out for dinner tomorrow night? No ties, no commitments. Just dinner. Wear something like that stripy top.

I couldn't help smiling. Alex was such a laugh – and such a friend! I quickly created a little design of a stylish couple drinking cocktails, with the words *See you at eight* inscribed underneath. I sent it to him as a PDF, which I knew would drive him crazy. Alex could barely type an email without calling for help. It would take him ages to work out how to download it. But then he'd be really pleased. And that would be the beginning of life without James.

The date with Alex went fine except for one troubling thing. As I was getting ready, I decided to put on my special football earrings: the gold ones. The ones I hadn't worn since the last time I'd gone out with James, and had taken off just before we'd made love. It was another step towards putting him right out of my mind.

But when I went to my special jewellery box, nestling in the satin bed was only one gold football. I couldn't understand it. Everything else was there – my diamanté drops, the silver necklace that Great Aunt Judy gave me, a few rings, nothing very valuable. But only one football.

I spent ages looking for it, in vain. It was gone. Somehow, it had disappeared. And yet I knew I'd put back both earrings after the last time I'd worn them. I remembered every single detail of the events of that magical night. I started to think I must be going mad, that perhaps I'd secreted it away in my sleep, or even that I'd sent it to James and forgotten all about it.

Then I noticed something else. Next to the jewellery box in my dressing-table drawer I kept a special make-up bag. It contained things like my sparkly nail varnish and some very expensive eye shadows as well as a few sachets of night cream and masks. One of the mask sachets had been opened and the cream was oozing out all over the bag. That was a shock. It hadn't been like that last time I'd looked in the drawer, I was sure of it. And more than that – it was a mask I'd used once before, and it had given me a rash. I'd decided to avoid it in future. It wasn't me who'd opened it, I was sure of that. Someone had done it on purpose. Someone had been poking around in my flat, and it was really beginning to spook me out.

I forced myself to be bright and chatty with Alex. Well, I couldn't tell him what was really going on, could I? First of all, it would mean confiding in him about James, which I wasn't about to do. Then it would mean telling him my suspicions about Holly, who was not only my friend but also his best friend's girlfriend. I didn't think it would go down very well if I explained why I thought she had it in for me – what I'd said to make her so upset. The more I thought about it, the more I realized that this whole tangled mess was something I simply had to keep to myself.

So we went out for a curry, kept our conversation fun and light, and I didn't think he had a clue that anything was bothering me at all.

But I was wrong. As we drew up outside the flat, he didn't wait to be invited in, merely turned off the engine, got out of the car and followed me upstairs.

As soon as we were inside, he grasped me by the shoulders and turned me to face him.

"Katie, why have you closed up again?" he asked. "Look, if there's something wrong, tell me. I'm your friend, I hope. I want to get near you. But I'm beginning to think that's something you just don't allow."

I smiled falsely. "That's not true," I told him. "Or maybe it's a little bit true. I – I'm not very good at opening up. But I do like you, Alex. I want to get to know you."

"Do you?" he asked, staring straight into my eyes. I nodded, willing it to be true. It would be so wonderful, so simple, to settle for a guy like him.

"Then you have to be straight with me," he said. "I'm not asking for much. I told you – no ties, no commitments. But I do like straight dealing."

"OK," I whispered. "I'll try."

"I don't believe you," he said, then pulled me into his arms and kissed me fiercely before turning away abruptly and slamming the door behind him.

Eleven

It had taken for ever to get to sleep. I couldn't stop thinking about all the terrible, spiteful things that had been happening. And worst of all, I found myself reliving over and over again those last moments with Alex – that fierce, bitter kiss. What if things had changed between us? What if all that easy friendship had been destroyed?

So when I arrived at the office the next morning I was relieved to find that Alex was almost like his old self.

"Hey, what's the capital of Peru?" he yelled as I walked through the door.

"Lima," I answered as I turned on my computer.

"Naa – can't be. That's an animal, isn't it? Like a camel but no humps."

"That's a llama," I corrected him, laughing.

"Is it?" he asked, looking crestfallen.

"Why d'you want to know?" I asked. He brandished a

glossy men's magazine at me – one of those ones that always has Jordan or Britney on the cover, usually in their underwear.

"It's this quiz," he explained. "You can win a laptop or a trip to New York."

"Cool," I commented. "What d'you have to do? Find out five ways to insult women in each major capital city? List your favourite women with reasons why they'd never go out with you? Or do you just have to talk about your feelings, for once? That would rule out most of the readers, for a start."

"Wrong, completely wrong," sang out Alex triumphantly. "That just goes to show how little you know about these magazines. They're far more sophisticated than you think."

"Oh, really?" I answered. "Don't tell me. You also have to list the world's ten sexiest meals and say how you'd get a girl to cook them for you."

"Wrong again. This is a tough general knowledge quiz – a hundred questions about areas that men about town like me should really know their way around."

"Let's see now – would that be football, cars and quantum physics?" I teased.

"Enough!" Alex shouted, throwing a box of paper clips at me. I ducked and they went all over the floor. Our heads knocked together as we bent to pick them up and we both laughed. It wasn't exactly intimate, but it was a start.

"OK," I conceded while I made the coffee, "tell me some of the questions and maybe I can help."

Soon the whole office was joining in, shouting out impossible answers to Alex's desperate pleas.

"What's the name of the sea that lies between Israel and Egypt?"

"The Black Sea," shouted someone. "No, the Red Sea!" and then everyone was yelling out different colours until Margaret Simpkins, one of the bosses, came out of her office to find out what all the fuss was about.

Alex was clearly obsessed with finishing the quiz and winning the prize. He was poring over the cinema section during the coffee break, banging his fist on his head. "I don't know any of these," he kept saying distractedly.

"What you need is my *Film Guide*," I told him. And that was when he begged me to go and get it during the lunch hour.

"Can't it wait until tomorrow?" I demurred.

"It could, but I'd rather it didn't," he pleaded. "Look – if you go and get it at lunchtime I'll buy you a sandwich for when you get back. And then I can carry on this evening. And – tell you what! If I'm still stuck we can tackle it together tomorrow night, in the pub."

This was his way of making peace, I realized. He wanted us to be friends again. He was actually asking me to go to the pub on Friday night as usual. So I smiled, and agreed to go and get the book if it meant that much to him. And when he smiled back, and assured me that it did, I somehow knew it wasn't just the book he was talking about . . .

So now here I was, barely an hour later, standing outside my own front door. But instead of unlocking it and bursting in to get the book and rush back to the office, I just stood there trembling, as a chill of fear crept down my spine. Something was wrong. The door was very slightly open, just a crack. I remembered locking it that morning, just as I always did.

Of course, it was sheer luck that I was here at home in the middle of the day. Sheer luck that today of all days I'd happen upon an intruder, a burglar, a persecutor – I didn't like to think who or what. What mattered was that someone was in there. And I was going to have to find out who, no matter what it cost me . . .

Oh well! I told myself with a shrug. There was no choice really. I just had to pluck up all my courage, fling open my own door and confront whoever it was prowling round my apartment.

I took a deep breath, counted to three – and went in. Actually, it was more like creeping in, but at least I'd managed it. I took a look round the kitchen/living-room. There were no signs that anyone had been there. Nothing was disturbed.

Then I edged my way to the bedroom. I inched round the door. At first glance, it looked just the way it always did. Then I looked again – and gasped. There was an ugly streak of red on the dressing-table mirror. I moved towards it and realized it was a message, scrawled in my own lipstick:

KEEP YOUR HANDS OFF!

Blinking back the tears of horror and fear I forced myself to read the message again. And again. Someone was out to get me – someone who knew where I worked and who'd found a way in to where I lived. Holly! Oh Holly! How could she hate me this much?

It was strangely quiet, I realized. Either Holly had gone, carelessly leaving the door ajar, or she was still here, lying in wait, or maybe just hoping I'd go away without finding her. I thought quickly. My flat was so tiny there were hardly any places to hide. There was only really one place she could be.

Very, very quietly I tiptoed out of the bedroom towards the final door. My fingers closed round the handle and, with a sudden, decisive movement, I threw open the door to the bathroom. It was empty! How could it be?

Then I noticed the telltale shake of the shower curtain, half-closed round the bath. I grabbed it and ripped it to one side. There, cowering in the bath, was a huddled figure. She wasn't Holly. That was what registered first. Then I realized I knew her. I recognized her. Hers was a face that had haunted

111

me, taunted me, lurked in the corner of my mind so very many times, waiting to torment me.

She had blonde, spiky hair and skin-tight jeans. Under her leather jacket was the tiniest of T-shirts, showing an awful lot of taut, skinny midriff. Her eyes were wide and terrified. She was not a burglar, not a wild axe woman, not a ghost and not even threatening. But as I came face to face with the woman who had tracked me down, stalked me, hounded and terrorized me, I can honestly say I was more scared than if she'd been a complete stranger out to kill me.

It was like coming face to face with my destiny. And now I had nowhere to run.

Twelve

For a few seconds we just stared at each other, neither of us quite capable of uttering a word. Then, after what seemed like an eternity, I whispered: "What are you doing here?"

The girl fixed me with a glazed expression, her eyes enormous in her pale, pointed face. Eventually, she uncurled and stepped out of the bath. Standing, she was taller than I was and very thin. Especially as she was wearing four-inch spiky heels.

"I'll explain," she said shortly. "I don't expect you to get it, but I'll try."

"Be my guest," I gestured wearily, leading her to the living-room.

As if in a trance, I made a pot of tea. I even put out some chocolate biscuits on a tray, with the milk jug. It occurred to me that this was a pretty strange scenario – me handing a cup of tea to the woman who'd just broken into my flat, intent on vandalizing it, as if she was a neighbour popping in to borrow a bowl of sugar.

"OK," she said, after she'd sipped her tea thoughtfully for a few moments. "I've been trying to warn you off. Simple as that."

"Warn me off what, exactly?" I asked, knowing the answer but praying that I might be wrong, that the whole thing might be a huge misunderstanding. That somehow this wasn't about James, after all.

But I knew her answer before she even spoke.

"Don't play the innocent little girl," she scoffed. "Believe me, I know you've tried that one. James's told me all about that little ploy."

"James . . ." I stammered. "He's told you about me?"

"Oh, sure," the girl nodded, her eyes narrowing as if the memory was painful, somehow. As if it was something she hadn't really wanted to know. "He tells me most things, you know."

"Why?" I asked simply, not really wanting to know the answer. And sure enough, when it came it was like a knife slicing through my heart, making me shudder with pain.

"He's my boyfriend," she said. "We've known each other quite a while, but we had a bit of a bust-up a few months ago and decided to cool it. We got back together a few weeks ago, not long after you ran into him."

I didn't want to hear about this but I had to.

"So you know that he and I—?"

"Of course I do," she broke in. "I know you went out with him. More to the point, I know you just wouldn't let him go. And I wasn't having that, not once he'd come back to me."

"So you admit that note and the Wasp Woman card were from you," I prompted her.

A faint smile spread over her face. "Yeah – that was good, wasn't it? Not very nice, I suppose, to be on the receiving end. I thought if I made it nasty enough it'd be effective. I was wrong though, wasn't I? That very day you came after him at the Dudlace grounds. Good job those bouncers were on hand, wasn't it? Good job I was there to call on them when they were needed."

So it was this girl – this spiteful, scheming girl – who'd had me led away from the grounds so humiliatingly. It wasn't James at all. I wondered what else she'd done on his behalf.

"I bet you wrote that note too, didn't you?" I said, thinking aloud. "It wasn't James at all."

She smiled again. "Let's just say I had a hand in it, yes. But don't kid yourself. James wanted you out of his life. I just helped with the wording."

Now, I suppose you're thinking at this point that I should have been devastated. But although it was pretty nasty coming face to face with James's new girlfriend, it wasn't quite as terrible as all that. Because sitting with her, listening to her tale of anguish and revenge, I began to realize that I wasn't the only one to be suffering this pain and jealousy. She was feeling it too. She felt threatened by me. That's why she'd gone to such lengths to get rid of me.

"So – what's your name?" I asked, pouring another cup of tea, trying not to react to her cruel words.

She grinned – the ghost of a smile. "I'm Charlotte – Charlotte Peach." She held out her hand and I shook it solemnly.

"Erm . . . pleased to meet you," I said, embarrassed. We both laughed. "I guess you know who I am," I added.

"Only too well," she acknowledged. "For someone who only went out with him a couple of times, you seemed to crop up everywhere."

"Did I?" I prompted her, genuinely intrigued. "How do you mean?"

Her face hardened. "Oh, you want a running tally, do you? Let's see now. Just after James and I got back together I found these under his pillow." She burrowed in the pocket of her shiny leather jacket and pulled out a pair of black lacy knickers – the ones I'd discarded the night I'd offered to cook for him and ended up in his bed.

"Fortunately for me, you left something else as well," she added, flourishing a piece of paper in front of me. I recognized it at once. It was the note I'd left him with my address and number on it. I'd even left my work number in case he wanted to contact me during the day.

"That's what gave me the idea of scaring you off, really," Charlotte mused. "He didn't want your number so I decided I could use it."

"So that's how you found out where I worked," I breathed, almost relieved to have got to the bottom of some of the mystery.

"Right – and I sent you that email from the Print Shop near where I work, so it couldn't be traced back to me," she said, looking pleased with herself.

An idea was beginning to take shape right at the back of my mind. It wasn't clear, it wasn't fully formed yet, but it was there and it gave me the strength to continue. I even managed to smile as I offered her a biscuit.

"So where do you work, then?" I asked chattily.

"Me? Oh, I'm a graphic designer. I work for a design agency in town: Brown and Black. Do you know them?"

I didn't, but I wasn't going to let her see that. I looked impressed. "Wow! What a great job! No wonder James likes you. Listen, Charlotte, I honestly didn't know he had a new girlfriend. If I had, I would never have tried to get back together with him. I'm not that kind of girl at all."

Charlotte's face softened. "Really?" she asked. "I thought everyone knew we were together. I mean, that night you gave him his organizer back – you must have seen us then."

With a renewed stab of pain I remembered that evening, remembered seeing that blonde, skinny figure hovering round James. So that was what was going on!

I shook my head. "I didn't know, or I would never have done it."

"Ah, yes – that message really freaked him out, you know? I mean, his organizer's really private. He felt terrible, thinking some stranger had written in it. It was like a burglar leaving graffiti on the wall. That's why I wanted to hurt you back, just the way you'd hurt him."

Again I willed myself not to react to what she was telling me, forced back the bitter tears that threatened to spill out on to my tight, smiling cheeks.

"Tell me, Charlotte, how did you manage to get into the flat? I mean, I can see how you did the email, the Wasp note, the smelly toe rag."

She giggled at that. "Oh, right. Sorry about that one. It was a bit childish, wasn't it?"

I ignored that, and carried on steadily: "But how did you get in?"

"Oh, that was easy," she said dismissively. She brought out a credit card and waved it in front of me. "This was all it took. Someone showed me how, once. A boyfriend who'd fallen into some unsavoury company. I sort of went off him when I realized how he made the money for his Versace jacket and Harley Davidson, but I remembered his little tip. Once you've got the knack, there's nothing to it. Unless people have reinforced locks. That's what I'd advise you to get now, by the way. Your security's terrible."

"So it would appear," I remarked drily. "So do you make a habit of breaking into people's homes and stealing their jewellery and vandalizing their furniture, or did I just strike lucky?"

Charlotte laughed, a little ashamed. "No, you're the only one. I – I maybe got a bit carried away. I didn't realize you were so – so nice," she admitted.

Good, I thought triumphantly. She's falling for it.

"I'm not that nice," I replied, composing my face into a sad, wistful expression. "I'm just normal, like you – a normal girl who wanted a guy who didn't want her. But now I know he's got someone else it makes all the difference."

"Does it?" Charlotte asked eagerly. "I'm so pleased." There she went again, revealing how scared she was of losing James, showing so plainly what a threat she thought I was. She was playing right into my hands.

"Don't worry," I said cosily. "I wouldn't dream of getting between James and the woman he really wants."

Well, that was true. It all depended on your interpretation, really.

"Oh Katie, that makes me feel terrible!" blurted out

Charlotte, all weepy and guilty, suddenly. "You seem so reasonable and nice – I can't believe I've done all these terrible things to you. Were you really upset?"

"A bit," I admitted, deliberately letting my voice wobble. "Especially – today."

Charlotte leaped up. "I'll clear it up right away," she offered. "Leave it to me. Oh, and by the way—" Again she fumbled in her pocket – and brought out my missing gold earring.

"I may be a vandal and a stalker but I'm not a thief," she said, thrusting it into my hand. We both laughed, and she threw her arms round me in a spontaneous hug. It was all I could do not to be sick.

"I'm sorry, Katie – really, really sorry. I must have been crazy to persecute you like that."

"Love makes us all do crazy things," I mumbled, watching as she set about cleaning up my dressing-table and polishing the mirror. Suddenly I thought of something else – something that had been preying on my mind ever since Charlotte had introduced herself.

"Did you say your surname was Peach?" I asked. She nodded.

"It's a bit unusual, isn't it? I used to hate it until I met James. But he loves it. He's always referring to me as his fruitcake, calling me the apple of his eye and his bowl of cherries. You know – because of Peach."

That's why it rang such a bell, I realized. The girl who'd sent in that request to his radio show! He'd called her a fruity dish, and said she'd made a plum choice. It was all falling into place.

"Yes, he's always making jokes about me being a peach of a girl," Charlotte let on obligingly, "especially on his show. It's his way of letting me know he's thinking about me."

She looked all dreamy and I wanted to kick her in the head. But instead I smiled and nodded indulgently. And all the while I was formulating this plan – this big plan. Even as we were chatting, I'd begun to work out how to get James back again. It was easy. All I needed to do was to make him realize who he really loved. Who he'd loved all along. If only Charlotte hadn't come along and spoilt it all! Charlotte had every reason to be worried about me, now more than ever. Because now she was on the way out.

Thirteen

"Who said 'Play it again, Sam' in what movie?" Alex asked, shouting above the Friday night racket down at the Queen's Arms.

"Trick question," I answered immediately. "The film was *Casablanca*, and it was Humphrey Bogart who wanted to hear his special song. But he never said 'Play it again, Sam.'"

"Wow, you're good!" whistled Alex admiringly. "I don't know why I ever needed your reference book. All I need is you. Oh, but hang on – that was only the first part of the question. The next one is, 'Who starred in the film *Play It Again, Sam*?'"

"Woody Allen," I yawned. "This is easy-peasy."

"Not for me it isn't," said Alex. "Now you're getting me really worried. Suppose I win the laptop? How could I possibly keep it, knowing you've answered so many of the questions?"

"I'll do a deal," I promised. "Keep the laptop if you win it, but you'll have to take me to New York if you win that trip instead."

"Done!" Alex beamed. "Now for Part Three. 'In which movie did the characters have an argument about the ending of Part One?' What on earth can that mean?"

"Well, the movie mentioned in Part One is *Casablanca*," I said thoughtfully. "So, let's see now – oh, of course! *When Harry Met Sally*. Billy Crystal and Meg Ryan have this argument about whether Ingrid Bergman was right to get on the plane with Victor."

Alex looked baffled. "Who? What? How do you know all this stuff anyway?"

I smiled, trying to look mysterious. I certainly wasn't planning to let on that the reason I knew so many films so intimately was that I'd spent so many lonely Saturday nights staying in with a box of chocolates and a nice weepy dvd. I didn't want him knowing my life had been so sad up until recently.

It was Friday night and Alex and I were out together – well, not alone together. The rest of the office were there too, and Sam and Holly. But it was the closest we'd been to a date since last week's awkward meeting. I knew this was my chance to make up with Alex, to make him like me again, and I was determined that this time I wouldn't throw it away.

Oh, it wasn't that I really wanted to go out with him, even

though I had to admit he was really good company, really sweet. But he wasn't James. There was no passion there for me, only a lukewarm sort of affection. But I needed Alex. I needed him for my big plan – my plan to get Charlotte out of the way so that James and I could be together again.

To do that, I needed to know as much as I possibly could about Charlotte's movements, her habits, her tastes. I'd stopped my charm offensive, trying to show James how much I loved him and how much he needed me. Instead, my new campaign was just about to get underway: Campaign Charlotte. And it was going to be so much easier to pull off if I had a boyfriend to go round with, to go to all the places where I might catch a glimpse of Charlotte and James together, or Charlotte alone.

So now, smiling happily at Alex as though nothing could make me happier than being in his company, I said brightly: "Look – I'll admit it. I'm a bit of a movie buff. I've got all those films on dvd at home. Why don't you come back with me tonight and we can watch them?"

"All of them?" asked Alex faintly.

'Why not?" I said gaily. "A triple bill. You get the popcorn, I'll provide the drinks."

"OK," agreed Alex. He looked puzzled but pleased. "What about the others? Maybe Holly and Sam would like to come too."

I flashed a quick look at Holly. She grinned and gave me a secret little wave.

"Why don't you ask them?" I said sweetly, but I knew what the answer would be. Holly and I had had lunch that very day – and we now understood each other very well indeed . . .

It had been a bit strained at first, after we'd sat down at Joe's Café and ordered our lunch. But then I plunged in, knowing that it was really up to me to get over this awkwardness.

"Listen, Holly, I owe you an apology. I really do. I was completely out of line last week. I should never have said those things about Sam. You know I didn't mean them."

Holly smiled her sweetest smile. "I know, Katie – you don't even need to say it. You were upset, that was all. And I shouldn't have said half those things either. It was me that upset you."

"So we're friends again?" I said hopefully.

"Of course we are," Holly assured me. "I never stopped being your friend, Katie. But there's just something I need to get straight. You know, on the phone you said some very strange things. Almost as if you were accusing me of something . . ."

"Oh, that," I hedged. "Well, this could all be a gigantic misunderstanding, but when I asked you what you thought you were doing last Saturday, what did you think I meant?"

Just then our food arrived, and Holly speared her potato thoughtfully a couple of times before she replied. "Well, at the time I assumed you meant that business with Alex."

"I'm sorry?" I asked. "What business?"

She sighed. "I was afraid you hadn't realized what had happened. Look, didn't you think it was a bit of a coincidence, Alex arriving at your door like that?"

"Not really," I shrugged. Then a slow realization began to dawn on me. "Are you telling me you had something to do with it?"

Holly grinned. "Just a bit," she admitted. "Look, after you stormed out I felt really bad. I knew you'd been hurt by James and everything, but I thought that now it was over, Alex might have a chance with you after all. So – so I rang him and told him to get round to your place at once."

"But why?" I wanted to know, still baffled.

"Oh, I just thought if he turned up while you were still in a state he'd be in a better position to – to make an impact on you, I suppose."

"But he was all oily," I protested. "He'd been under a car changing a wheel. You call that sexy?"

We both laughed, then. "Well," Holly went on, "he did say he'd been trying to fix his car, and I thought that would be a really good excuse to call on you. You know – as if he'd just happened to break down in your road."

"You mean, there was no breakdown?"

She nodded. "That's right. No breakdown, no puncture. He was just working on the car and I sort of sent him over. You're not cross, are you?"

"No, just confused," I answered, forking a dollop of cheese and sweetcorn filling into my mouth. As I chewed, Holly seemed to be puzzling over something.

"So if you didn't know I'd set that up, what were you talking about on the phone?" she demanded at last. "What was it you thought I'd done?"

So I took a deep breath and told her everything. About the nasty message I'd received that day, alongside the awful letter from James. About the humiliation of being dragged away from him and booted out of the football grounds. And then I went through the whole catalogue of horrible things that had followed – the email on my screen, the smelly rag pushed through my door, the missing earring and then, finally, yesterday's confrontation with Charlotte.

She listened with widening eyes, as if I'd been telling her a horror story. I must say, it was beginning to feel like one. I'd lived through a nightmare of being persecuted and terrorized and somehow, now that I was sharing it with a friend, it all felt even worse.

"But surely you couldn't have thought I'd do any of those

spiteful things?" Holly said indignantly. "I mean – that's sick, it really is."

"I didn't want to think you could, Holly," I said quietly. "But I couldn't think who else was so angry with me – who else even knew that much about me. And I felt so guilty about upsetting you, I started to think I deserved to be punished."

"Oh, rubbish!" Holly said briskly. "I didn't take it seriously. I trust Sam and he trusts me. But I was just worried about you, that was all. I could see how upset you were, and that was why you were trying to hurt me. I'd never, ever do anything like that, believe me."

"I know," I said wearily. "I know that now. And I feel even worse for suspecting you in the first place. I'm sorry, Holly – really sorry." Suddenly, I felt the hot pricking of tears welling in my eyes and then they began to roll uncontrollably down my cheeks.

"Oh, no! Oh, please don't cry," Holly pleaded, fumbling in her bag for tissues. Instead, out fell a half-eaten packet of Starburst and a Mars Bar.

Eventually, she brought out a slightly used tissue and began to mop ineffectually at my face. Despite my tears, I began to laugh.

"I'm sorry, I don't know why I'm crying," I mumbled. "I never do."

"Well, maybe that's part of your problem," Holly suggested

shrewdly. "You bottle up your feelings too much, Katie, and then they come out in weird ways, like that whole business with James. Instead of pretending everything was OK, and trying to get back together with him, it would've been so much better to have had a good cry, admit you'd been hurt and then carry on with real life."

I didn't reply. I had a horrible feeling she might have a point. But then I remembered that look of dread and anxiety on Charlotte's face – remembered that it was Charlotte, not James, who'd been keeping us apart. Holly was wrong, I told myself firmly. She just didn't realize how special it was between me and James – how powerful the feelings were. This was no ordinary love but something sent down from heaven. And nothing, no one, was going to stand in our way.

"Well, at least you know now," Holly was saying, cutting into my day-dream.

"Know what?" I asked, realizing I'd missed some of the conversation.

"You know what it feels like to be the target of someone else's obsession," Holly said, stirring her coffee as if she'd rather look at that than at me. "What Charlotte did to you was completely out of line. It was nasty and vindictive and scary, right?"

I nodded. Of course, Holly was right. I'd been terrified for days, living in dread of the next ugly act, the next intrusion.

"But then, what you were doing to James was pretty sick too," Holly went on bravely. She definitely wasn't wanting to look at me as she spoke. I watched her pouring a third sachet of sugar into her coffee. I didn't even think she took sugar!

"But that was completely different," I protested. "I wasn't trying to hurt him. All I was doing was reminding him of our good times. They were messages of love, not hate."

Holly shook her head sadly. "All the same," she said, "they must have been very unnerving to receive. What he was getting was your obsession with him, Katie, don't you see? You were stalking him. And being stalked isn't very nice."

I fell silent. I hadn't thought about it that way at all. I certainly hadn't connected Charlotte's actions and my own. Charlotte had been conducting a campaign of intimidation against me. It was terrible to think that that might have been how James saw me.

Then I realized with blinding clarity what the difference was. Of course! It wasn't James who felt threatened and intimidated by me, it was Charlotte. All I'd offered James was love and devotion, and that was what Charlotte couldn't stand.

"So you won't pursue him any more, will you?" persisted Holly. "You don't want to be branded a stalker, do you?"

I shook my head and smiled. "I promise I won't go after

James any more," I told her. "I'll leave him alone. No more messages. No more following."

And it was completely true. From now on, it wasn't James I'd be stalking, it was Charlotte. Once she was out of the way James would come back to me – I just knew he would.

"So how about you and Alex?" Holly went on. "He really likes you, you know. And he's such a lovely bloke. All he wants is to get to know you a bit – to give it a try."

"I know," I told her earnestly. "And that's what I want too. Of course, we're going to take it very slowly. I don't want to get involved too soon after what happened with James . . ." My voice dropped, and Holly instantly looked sympathetic.

"Of course," she said. "I think you're being really sensible. Katie, you haven't been out with that many boys, have you?"

I didn't answer immediately. I was startled by her accuracy. "Is it so obvious?" I asked eventually, unable to look up from my coffee and aware that I was blushing.

"Look, there's no need to get defensive about it," Holly said at once. "I just got the feeling it was all a bit new to you. I mean, you've changed so much in the past few weeks. You used to look – well . . ."

"A bit dorky," I suggested ruefully. "I know. I suppose I hadn't really given much thought to the way I looked up till then. I just assumed I was fat and plain because my mum always told me I was."

Holly looked shocked. "Really? Funny sort of thing for a mother to say. Mine's always telling me I'd look really pretty if I got the hair out of my face and stopped wearing all that gloomy black."

"You're lucky," I said sincerely. "She sounds great, your mum."

"Oh, she's OK," Holly said affectionately. "Terrible taste in music, of course, and I can never borrow her shoes because she believes high heels cripple you later in life. But apart from that she's pretty good. And Sam adores her."

"Does he?" I asked, amazed, thinking about my own mother, who was so quick to sniff disapprovingly at anything unfamiliar or new. "I just couldn't imagine introducing a boy to my mum. If she met James she'd probably die on the spot from shock."

"How about Alex?" prompted Holly.

I thought for a moment, then shook my head. "No, she'd probably hate him, too. She'd hate the idea of me even having a boyfriend and she'd be amazed that anyone would want to go out with me. It's probably safest to keep them well away from her."

'Well, anyway, you're not exactly serious about him, are you?" Holly said. "And that's what I was going to say, Katie. You should try just enjoying yourself for a bit. Go out with Alex but don't expect it to get all intense and committed. You need to learn to have fun."

"OK," I consented, smiling. "Fun it is. From now on I'm going to concentrate really, really hard on having fun and I'm seriously going to relax. Are you happy?"

Holly laughed. "I just want you to be happy," she said. "You and Alex . . ."

Late that Friday night we sat curled up side by side on the sofa, watching all my weepiest old dvds. I was quietly sobbing while Alex handed me tissues.

"So nice to see you enjoying yourself," he commented.

"I am," I insisted. "You're supposed to cry at this bit. That's what it's for."

"Right," said Alex, screwing his face into a look of intense concentration as Humphrey Bogart made his famous goodbye speech to Ingrid Bergman at the airfield in *Casablanca*.

"No, it's no good, I can't seem to sob," Alex said. "Maybe I shouldn't have held my breath for so long. I feel gaspy but not weepy."

I giggled through my tears, loving his silliness. It was like that with Alex. He could make me laugh by uttering total nonsense. He looked pleased, and snuggled closer to me, his arm creeping round my shoulders.

"This is nice," he said simply. I nodded.

"Really nice," he added, then very gently, very slowly he kissed me.

"Really, really nice," he murmured. And then he was kissing me harder, his lips pressing mine more and more urgently until I found myself responding, kissing him back, my arms twined round his neck and pulling him down towards me.

Still locked in a passionate embrace we slid slowly down into the sofa until I was lying full length, with Alex above me, his body crushing mine, as his hands travelled up and down and then, finally, underneath my back, pulling me closer and closer against him.

I gasped, urging him to touch me, arching my back so that I was thrusting against him, my head thrown back in abandon as his lips bruised my neck. Then, very gently, he began to lift my T-shirt, his hands coming into contact with my hot skin.

Immediately, I tensed up and very slightly shrank away from him.

"Katie?" he asked tenderly. "What's wrong? Tell me."

I shook my head, not even sure myself of the complex web of feelings that churned inside me. "It's too soon," I explained weakly. "I – I'm not ready for this."

Alex stared at me, his face hot with desire. Then he pulled down my T-shirt and sat up.

"OK," he said. "You're probably right. We shouldn't rush into anything. And – and I respect your feelings, Katie." Then he grinned. "But that doesn't stop me fancying you like crazy. You are one hot lady, you know that?"

I smiled, unable to say anything at all.

"So I think I'd better go, before anything else happens. Call you soon, OK?"

With that, he was gone, leaving me trembling with a confused mixture of desire and relief. It was James I wanted, I was sure of that. James who turned me on, made my senses sing, filled my dreams. Alex was just someone to pass a little time with until I was reunited with my true, my perfect love. So how come, just now, for those few heady moments, I'd experienced such a dizzying rush of desire for him?

Fourteen

A whole week had gone by before Holly and I met up for lunch again. By now, my plan was well underway. And Holly had no idea that she was taking part in it, although she did grumble a bit about my choice of restaurant.

"Why are you dragging me all this way?" she complained, stopping to adjust the strap on her very new, very high heels. "When you said a snack at lunchtime I thought you meant a trip to a sandwich bar, not a trip to Birmingham. On foot. Ouch!" She rubbed her ankle, which had just given way.

"Not much further," I told her cheerfully, marching on ahead. I wasn't really lying – unless you think three more streets is a long way. I was just minimizing the blow.

"I hope it's going to be worth it," Holly panted, tottering after me with a pained look on her face. "I mean, I don't know what's so wrong with Joe's Café in the High Street."

"Oh, live a little, why don't you?" I said. "Learn to enjoy

adventures. Look, I'm taking you to a nice, new, trendy place to brighten up your week. Give you something different to talk about."

"It'll be really different if I break my ankle and end up in Casualty," Holly muttered. "All those nice doctors to chat up, and horribly injured people."

"Here we are!" I announced at last, relieved.

The Grape Vine was one of those trendy wine bars, with very white walls and plain wooden tables. It wasn't exactly glamorous, but it was obviously where the smart set liked to have their brunch meetings. The place was full of cool people in sunglasses.

We found a table for two and squeezed ourselves between a party of very loud guys on one side, and a couple of girls just behind us. One of them was very familiar. I would have recognized that bright blonde spiky hair anywhere. And that pointed little elfin face.

It wasn't surprising really. I'd asked for a table by the window, knowing it would be near where Charlotte liked to sit. Of course, I couldn't be sure that we'd be right next to her. That was pure luck. But I was fairly certain we'd be close enough for me to see her, watch her, learn even more about her.

I'd been working on Operation Charlotte for nearly a week

now. And I'd found out quite a bit. First of all, I'd discovered where she worked and had hung around outside. It was way up this side of town, but designers start later and finish later than estate agents, so I had plenty of time to pack up after work and make my way to her office.

That first Monday evening I waited around for nearly an hour, staring into a jeweller's window and checking my watch ostentatiously from time to time to show I was waiting for someone. Then, just as I was about to give up she emerged, chattering loudly to some friend of hers with bright red hair and the tiniest skirt you ever saw, with fishnet tights and shiny boots.

I gave them a minute or two, just to make sure they hadn't spotted me. Then, feeling a bit like one of those detectives on TV, I followed them, nipping into doorways occasionally if it looked as though they might turn round. They didn't. They made their way to a wine bar a few streets away. After a moment or two, I slipped in behind them.

It was dark inside, the shutters were down and each table was lit by a candle in a bottle. So I was able to squash into a table close by, and while I sipped my mineral water I strained my ears to catch as much conversation as possible.

"So how's it going with Wonder Boy, then?" Red Hair asked, as soon as they'd settled down.

"Great," I managed to hear. "We're really getting on well.

You know, I think we're made for each other, we've got so much in common."

At that, I nearly choked on my water, sending peanuts flying in all directions. How could Charlotte possibly be so deluded? It was me James was made for – me who understood his thoughts, his dreams.

"Bit of a drag, though, all that football, football, football, isn't it?" asked the friend.

"Oh, not really," Charlotte replied rather smugly. "I mean, I wish we had more time to spend together, but I've got to accept the football because it's part of James and James is part of me. In fact, I'm getting to quite like it. It can be pretty exciting sometimes."

This time I really did splutter and cough. What a loser this girl was! How could she say such daft things about football? It wasn't something you could "quite like". It wasn't just a question of finding it exciting sometimes. Football had to be a passion, an overwhelming obsession. It had to be, if you were going out with a football player. More than ever, I was convinced that Charlotte couldn't be right for James. She didn't understand what made him tick.

"Well, has he scored yet?" giggled Red Hair. "How many goals has he got so far? And tell me; does 'Offside' mean what I think it does?"

They both burst into a peal of giggles, and Charlotte

lowered her voice so I didn't hear what she said next. I was quite relieved, really. It was one thing knowing she wasn't the right girl for James to end up with, but that didn't mean I wanted to hear the details about what they were doing together right now. It was too painful even to think about . . .

The rest of that week, following Charlotte began to become a way of life. I heard her arranging to have lunch with Red Hair the following day, in the Grape Vine. So I made a little trip there, just to check it out. I didn't eat there or anything, just hung around outside for a bit, quietly observing them through the window.

Charlotte was a picky eater, I noticed. She perused the menu for ages, then seemed to be engaged in a long, earnest conversation with the waiter before ordering. When her food arrived, I saw that she'd just got a plain salad, no dressing, and a glass of water.

Slimming, I thought triumphantly. That must be it! She may have a model's skinny figure but she certainly suffers to keep it that way. I was sure I was right later in the week, when I trailed her to the art gallery.

Well, this time it wasn't exactly trailing. I overheard her as I was dragging a reluctant Alex round some exhibition of photographs at the local museum and art gallery. It wasn't exactly a coincidence, either. That was a piece of luck, really After seeing her with her workmate I'd developed this burning curiosity about where she worked. She didn't call it an office. I'd heard them say they had to get back to the studio quite soon, that day they went out for lunch. I really wanted to know what a studio looked like.

So the next day, Wednesday, I suggested to Alex that we should think about smartening up our image. He was quite enthusiastic, and said I should talk to Margaret or Tom about it. They were always willing to listen to good ideas.

So I did. I found myself urging them to invest in a proper corporate image, with a new logo and lots of leaflets and impressive, heavy notepaper. I'd created a few designs on the computer first, just to give them an idea of what could be done.

"But this is absolutely marvellous, Katie!" said Margaret encouragingly. "Maybe we should get you to come up with the designs."

"No, this is just easy-peasy stuff, very basic," I told them, trying to sound knowledgeable. "There are much better things that real graphic designers do. Why don't I get together a few samples and estimates to give you an idea?"

They jumped at it. "Well done – for showing initiative," Tom said admiringly.

"I'm so pleased we've got you, Katie," Margaret added. "I don't know how we ever managed before."

So I'd got the go-ahead. And that very afternoon, slightly

disguised in sunglasses and a baseball cap, I found myself climbing the three steep flights to the offices of Brown and Black. Actually, my plan wasn't quite as watertight as I'd hoped. I was shown straight into the office of some very young guy – it was impossible to tell whether he was a director of the company or a trainee. Designers are a bit like that, I discovered.

He listened as I outlined what I thought Cherry and Simpkins needed.

"There are quite a few local estate agents, so we reckoned it would be useful to have a sharper style of branding," I explained. "Of course we're a good firm, the very best, but I don't feel our image does us credit. What we need is something to demonstrate that we have the cutting edge."

All the time I was talking, and he was nodding, and then after that while he was talking and bringing out samples, I felt myself getting more and more on edge. This was such a waste of time! Here I was, right in the lion's den, and I hadn't so much as glimpsed her.

My only break came when there was a knock on the door, and Charlotte herself popped her head round. She barely glanced at me, just said: "Sorry to interrupt. I didn't realize you had someone with you. I just wondered if you were coming to the exhibition tomorrow night. We thought we'd all go along, because Larry's got some pictures in it."

And she was gone. And soon after that, I gathered up all the leaflets and sample logos and other paraphernalia that the young man was urging me to take a look at. As I left, I glanced back and got a brief glimpse of a large, bright office with yellow walls and huge great desks and drawing boards. That was it. But I'd got something else, too: my next secret date with my prey.

Alex was surprised when I suggested going to the exhibition.

"That's not like you," he protested. "I thought you'd rather go to the cinema, or watch a rerun of the finals of the World Cup. Or – hey, did I tell you? I've got this new dvd of great soccer mistakes. We could get in a Chinese and—"

"That would be great," I said. "Football dvd second, photographs first."

"Do I have to?" Alex asked, looking like a sulky boy.

"No, of course not," I said. "It's up to you whether you want to expand your horizons or not. I'd heard it was quite an interesting exhibition, that's all. And it's all pictures of this area – taken by local photographers through the century. But if you'd rather go to the pub and cut yourself off from an interesting experience, don't let me stand in your way."

"OK, OK," he sighed. "You know, I think I liked you better the way you used to be, all shy and lumpy and not at all bossy."

"Thanks a lot," I snapped. I knew he was teasing but I just wasn't any good at accepting criticism. It was all too close to the truth for me to be able to laugh.

Actually, the exhibition was quite good. It was interesting to see all the streets and houses so familiar from our property lists and display windows, as they had been a hundred years ago, and then between the wars, right up to the present. Even Alex seemed to enjoy himself.

But I stopped concentrating as soon as I saw that familiar spiky blonde head appear in the doorway. Charlotte was wearing a bright pink jacket. You could always spot her in a crowd, which was useful for me. She was with a few friends from her office, chattering loudly away at them as usual.

"Seeing the Striker tonight, then?" Red Hair asked.

Charlotte shook her head. "Nope, he's at team practice again. It's a really busy time of year right now. Of course it'll ease up after April, but right now we can only see each other at weekends. And even then it's a bit tricky."

I thought my ears were going to burst, I was straining so hard to hear her.

"But he's so sweet," she went on. "If he's playing away, he tries to get back in the evening. But if it's too far away, he sometimes stays the night and arranges for me to meet him. Well, it's only been a couple of times. Once we stayed in a hotel in Leicester, which was quite fun. But the other time was much better. He found a little cottage in the country, and we had it all to ourselves for the weekend. It was so romantic . . . I'd love to do that again some time. But I think James really prefers the big hotels. He likes having a swim and using the gym. And he says he loves to be able to leave a pile of dirty towels, knowing someone else has to clear them up . . ."

I hated hearing all the intimate little details, but I made myself listen. This was important – all of it. The more I knew, the easier it would be to proceed with my plan.

I wanted to hang around and see what else I could glean, but Alex was getting restless.

"OK, it was good, but enough's enough," he said firmly. "Time for chow mein and prawn crackers now."

As he was dragging me out of the building, I overheard the guy I'd talked to that very afternoon. "Hey, who wants fish and chips?" he boomed.

"Not me," Charlotte replied at once. "I – I'm not that hungry."

Aha! I thought triumphantly. Slimming again! That girl is neurotic about her appearance. She must be starving herself.

And now it was Friday, and I'd managed to manoeuvre Holly into coming to this fancy restaurant with me so that I could do my spying at close quarters. I was wearing a wild velvet peaked cap that covered most of my face, and I kept on a pair of dark glasses right through the meal just to make sure my target wouldn't recognize me. I'd wondered if Holly would tease me about my new image but she was far too busy frowning over the hand-scrawled menu. I noticed that once again Charlotte was picking at a plain salad.

"What do you suppose they mean by wilted raddiccio with rocket and fried Halloumi?" Holly asked.

"No idea," I muttered. "I'm sticking to the omelette and chips."

Charlotte's mate was now wolfing down a double blackcurrant and caramel pancake for dessert. Charlotte was gazing at it with a mixture of horror and envy. She was sipping a black coffee.

"Go on, have a mouthful," Red Hair urged her.

But she shook her head with a little shudder. "You know I can't, Nicole," she said longingly. "You shouldn't tempt me."

Soon after that they left, and I was able to relax and chat normally to Holly. She had no idea why we'd come here, no idea that I'd been hanging on to every word, every move at the table behind us.

Now I could be myself again – whoever that was.

Fifteen

"Here we go, here we go, here we go!" we bellowed merrily, yelling out the words at the top of our voices. It was a brilliantly sunny spring morning, just a weekend later. The sky was a piercing blue, and as we scudded through the country roads the fields glistened with fresh new grass and burgeoning crops. Occasionally we'd pass the first lambs, gambolling unsteadily on their gangly legs, or cheerful bursts of daffodils on the hills around us.

As Alex started up yet another football chorus and I joined in with ear-splitting gusto, I realized I felt more alive than I had for weeks – ever since my love affair with James had started to fall apart. As we raced past the hedgerows and cruised through the pretty villages, I had to admit to myself that I felt almost happy.

Alex was easy to be with. He was great company. We were out on a jaunt. And, best of all, it was Monday morning and that made the whole trip feel even more exciting. I'd got so stuck in the routine of going to the office every day. It was really refreshing to be doing something different – and to imagine everyone else chained to their desks, opening the post and answering the phones, having problems with the computer and wrestling with the windows, which always seemed to stick on sunny days, turning the whole place into a greenhouse!

As it happened, Alex and I had spent the whole of Saturday together, and that was when we'd cooked up this plan for our awayday. I hadn't intended to let him assume we were going to see each other that regularly. In fact, I'd decided to ration our meetings so that he wouldn't get any wrong ideas. But in the end, I just got too depressed at the prospect of sitting in my flat all alone, rearranging my football albums or pasting cuttings about James in my scrapbook.

And it wasn't as if I was really leading Alex on, I reasoned with myself. We'd agreed to take things slowly, to get to know one another, to become friends. And what could be wrong with two friends going shopping together, cooking a meal, watching TV?

Of course, that wasn't quite all we did. We had a really good laugh on Saturday night trying to make pancakes. Alex insisted that we do it properly, and toss them in the pan. I had the first go.

"One, two, three, over!" he yelled. I flicked my wrist and managed to lift the pancake about a centimetre out of the pan before it flopped back again.

"Here, let me have a try," said Alex, snatching the heavy frying pan. He started to jiggle it up and down, bracing himself as if he was about to do a karate kick. Then, with a mighty effort, he raised the pan in one sudden movement. The pancake flew right up in the air – and plastered itself on the ceiling.

"I think all this cooking is a bit over your head," I laughed. Alex grinned facetiously.

"Very funny, I don't think!" he said. "Stop joking and pass me some more pancake mix. I think I'm getting the hang of this."

The next pancake flipped over, just the way it should, but instead of landing back in the pan it collapsed on the floor. Shaking with laughter, I bent down to try and scrape up the mess, without realizing that Alex had had the same idea. Our heads knocked together and we both went sprawling to the floor.

And from there, it just seemed the most natural step in the world to be locked in each other's arms, all thoughts of the pancakes forgotten.

"We could be doing this somewhere more comfortable," suggested Alex, breaking off from kissing me to remove bits of pancake from my hair. I think he must have felt me tense up in his arms. For a fleeting moment a shadow darkened his face, but then it was gone.

He got up abruptly. "I'd better go soon," he said, not really looking at me. "I've got work to do."

"On a Sunday?" I questioned him. I wondered whether he was just making an excuse to get away, now that I'd rebuffed him.

"Yeah, well, I've got some paperwork to do and I'll get really behind if I don't do it tomorrow. On Monday I've got to go all the way to Mansfield to look at a cottage some old lady's put on the market. It's bound to be a waste of a journey. I've seen so many of them – full of damp and covered in rotten ivy, with cherry trees in the garden that have eaten away at the foundations. Even if they get into our lists they're right at the bottom with lots of words like 'charming' and 'characterful' and 'rustic' – meaning 'in need of major renovation and likely to fall down.'"

"Mansfield," I repeated, frowning. Why was that name familiar? "Hey, that's the next village to Stoniton, isn't it? Where Great Aunt Judy lives."

I explained that I'd promised to look in on her cottage every so often and Alex got quite excited.

"Well, come with me then, and we'll do both," he suggested. "Margaret and Tom won't mind, I'm sure. I'll tell them I'm training you to look over potential houses. We'll go to Mansfield in the morning, then a pub lunch, then on to your cottage for the afternoon."

So that's where we were heading on that bright, blustery March morning. Alex's cottage in Mansfield was every bit as dilapidated and damp as he'd predicted. We clambered round it gloomily, trying to look for good points.

"The garden's got potential," I said, peering through a grimy kitchen window on to a patch of green overgrown with weeds, but with a couple of apple trees and the remains of some pretty shrubs.

"If you fancy a dandelion garden," muttered Alex. He was examining the wooden beams in the ceiling and reached up and tapped one gently with his hand. Immediately it crumbled and fell to the floor.

"Ripe for conversion," I said, laughing. "With many original features – if you don't count parts of the ceiling."

It didn't take long for us to inspect the rest of the cottage, and then we were off to Stoniton, where we sat in the garden of a quaint little village pub and ate huge slabs of bread and cheese and drank Coke out of ancient beer mugs. Then it was on to Great Aunt Judy's place.

"Now that's what I call a cottage!" Alex commented approvingly as we drew up before a small, neat little house in pale yellow stone, covered with ivy and with a winding path through a beautifully tended front garden.

Excitedly, I unlocked the front door, which opened into a lovely little old-fashioned parlour, with a window-seat, lots of comfortable armchairs and an open fireplace. We spent ages exploring the house – the farmhouse-style kitchen, the little cellar where Aunt Judy kept her home-made wines, the surprisingly fussy main bedroom, draped with satin and lace, and the spare room covered with wonderful framed family photographs and filled with completely surprising objects like an antique spinning wheel and a brand-new computer.

"She must be a character, your great aunt," Alex said admiringly. "How come you've never visited her before?"

I shrugged, embarrassed. "I – I'm not sure. She always visits us – that's the way it is. My mum probably wouldn't have let me, even if I'd wanted to come and see her. She's a bit . . . erm . . . set in her ways."

I didn't expect Alex to understand the sort of upbringing I'd had. I didn't really understand it myself. It was only since I'd left home and started to meet new people, see how they got on with life and with each other, that I realized how very different my own family life had been. Other people's mums wanted the best for their children. Mine seemed dedicated to preventing me ever doing anything at all.

"What's up, Katie?" Alex broke into my thoughts. "You look sad all of a sudden."

I turned to him, realizing my eyes were full of tears – tears of longing for a childhood I'd never had, for a love that maybe I'd never find.

"Come here," Alex said, and pulled me into his arms. For a few moments he held me close. Gratefully, I nestled in the comfort of his familiar embrace. Then, very gently, he kissed me. It felt so good, so natural, that I found myself responding, my arms creeping round his neck.

And soon, very soon, we were lying full length on the bed, and Alex's hands were roaming my body as his kisses became more insistent, his caresses more urgent. More than anything, I wished that I could love him. It would have been perfect.

But that treacherous image of James was just too strong. It was James I wanted to be lying with me now, kissing me, making love to me. And so, yet again, I pulled away from Alex, trying not to notice the pain in his eyes.

"Katie," he whispered, his voice harsh with passion, "you know I'm not going to rush you. You know I'd never do anything you didn't want."

I nodded.

"But I really like you," he went on. "I think you like me. And – I don't know how long I can go on like this . . ."

I thought quickly. The next stage of my plan was already forming in my head. I'd got to try and get James back. That was all I cared about – it was my mission, my obsession, my goal. I'd have to act soon, and I was going to be triumphant.

That was what I told myself. But until then, having Alex around was just too good to lose.

"Just give me a couple of weeks," I told him. "I – I think I'll be much more sure of where we both stand by then." And, strangely enough, my words were even truer than I realized . . .

Early that evening, as he was driving me home, Alex switched on the radio and a familiar velvety voice wafted over the crackly speaker. It was James, introducing his Monday night show. This time he'd devoted the whole programme to young players and he had a bunch of football maniacs from the local primary school in the studio.

As always, hearing his voice was enough to make my heart pound in a way that, somehow, Alex never could. As usual, I was a mixture of excitement, longing and a kind of terror. And then it all gave way to a shaft of pure jealousy.

One of the kids asked him how he spent his weekends.

"Oh, I eat a lot of fruit for breakfast," he began. That, of course, was a reference to Charlotte and her stupid surname. It was all part of their secret joke. "Then nothing else until after the match, because you can't play your best on a full stomach. Then I like to relax with a special person who's a bit of a peach and the apple of my eye."

Of course I knew it was just a bit of a laugh. It didn't mean he really liked Charlotte – not the way he'd liked me. But it

154

was still painful to listen to and I almost switched the radio off. But I was glad I didn't. I would have missed the most vital piece of information – the detail that would finally put my whole plan into operation.

It was simple, really. James was explaining that if he played away from home he'd sometimes stay away for Saturday night. And sometimes his girlfriend would come, too. Well, I knew all that already. But now he was saying that he had an away match coming up that very Saturday and he had plans to turn it into a really memorable weekend. Nothing special there, really. Except that then he mentioned the name of the other team: Middleton.

My heart gave a violent lurch. Middleton was about thirty miles from Dudlace – far enough away to justify an overnight stay. But that wasn't what interested me so much. What made me sit up with a jolt, my mind racing wildly, was that I'd seen Middleton mentioned that very morning, when we were leaving Stoniton. There it was, on a road sign – Middleton: twelve miles.

That meant that Aunt Judy's cottage was about midway between Dudlace and Middleton. And that gave me my best idea yet. It was going to be a real clincher.

Sixteen

Of course, when I'd first had the idea – the most daring, impossible, dangerous idea of all – I hadn't really imagined it could have worked out so brilliantly. It had started with that visit to the cottage with Alex. Then, when I heard James on the radio, I knew I had the perfect opportunity to get Charlotte out of the way and take her place. All it needed was a little careful planning, I thought, impressed at the boldness of it all. Then there I'd be, together with James once again, all barriers between us overturned. And then I'd know, once and for all, how much he really loved me.

So that very next day I began to make it happen. The first bit was easy. I rang the football club press office and put on a London drawl.

"Oh, hi! It's Diva here, from *Pizazz*. We're a new girls' magazine with attitude. I'm doing a report on up and coming stars and I quite fancy including James Angel. As it happens I'll be in Middleton on Saturday, which is just such a coincidence because I can't remember the last time I was out of London. Except to go to New York, of course; Anyhow, I thought it would be cool to do the interview after his match. Can you arrange that for me, love?"

It was amazing, really. I'd got far more confident than I'd ever been before I left home, but even the new me would never, ever dare to talk that way – not as me. But as soon as I pretended to be someone else, I found it was quite easy, which was just as well, considering what I was going to have to do next.

I rattled on for a bit, trying to sound bored and fashionably jaded, just as I imagined London magazine journalists would be. And to my amazement, the girl at the other end bought it. She believed me. And she told me exactly what I wanted to know. Yes, James Angel would be in Middleton for a match and yes, he'd be staying on afterwards at the Clarendon Hotel. She even gave me the room number. Perhaps I'd like to interview him at around five o'clock? She could try and arrange that if I wanted.

Of course I had no intention of making that particular date. But now that I knew where he was staying, the rest should be easy.

Alex was casting me a few odd looks across the office, so

for the next couple of hours I concentrated on work, trying to be super-efficient to show there was nothing sinister on my mind. Then, after I'd made everyone their mid-morning coffee, and handed out chocolate biscuits as a treat, I settled down to my next task, a tricky one.

Luckily I'd kept a few sheets of headed stationery from the local radio station, the night I'd helped out with James's show. We all had. It was like a souvenir. Now the notepaper was going to become a crucial accessory in my plot.

Discreetly, I managed to type a brief note on the computer and print it on to the paper without anyone noticing. It was short and to the point, rushed but affectionate.

Delicious Peach,
Can't wait to see you on Saturday. I've changed the
arrangements just for you. I've found us a country
cottage where we can be alone, right in the middle of
nowhere. Here's the address and a key in case you arrive
before I do. I'll be doing promo interviews and won't
make it before seven. Looking forward to a whole night
of cherry picking.

Then I just added *Love James,* in his handwriting. That wasn't hard. I knew it better than my own.

I was pleased with the letter. It had enough details to

convince Charlotte it was genuine, especially the fruity bits. I'd even managed to find out his movements for the week and knew for a fact he'd be in strict training and completely out of contact, so she wouldn't be able to get in touch with him to double-check the arrangements. And why should she doubt them, anyway? She'd be far too busy feeling smug, thinking he was prepared to give up a luxury hotel for a romantic little cottage, just to please her.

Well, I knew him better, didn't I? I understood his wants and needs as if they were my own. James was a sportsman heading for international stardom – the fast set, the big city, the happening things. If Charlotte wanted some nerd to pick hollyhocks and trample through mud with her, she'd picked the wrong guy.

Grinning, I slipped the extra key to Aunt Judy's cottage into the envelope with the letter and the address, then sealed it. I'd had the key cut on the way in to work. Charlotte was going to slip right into my trap. And even if she had her doubts and wanted to check the arrangements with James – well, that wasn't going to be very easy. When he was training nothing got in his way, not even his mother, definitely not a girlfriend. I knew all about that level of training. There were no phone-calls. No distractions. No chance at all of spoiling the final scene in my own little drama . . .

Then, almost as if I'd willed it to happen, I had another

stroke of luck. Ever since I'd told Alex to cool things for a week or two he'd kept out of my way – polite, friendly even, but certainly not intimate. But that very day, after lunch, he passed by my desk and stopped for a chat.

"How about coming to the match on Saturday?" he suggested casually. "The whole crowd is going."

"All the way to Middleton?" I exclaimed.

"It's not that far," Alex said. "We'll take two cars and make a day of it. Maybe go on to eat somewhere in town. Apparently they do the best Indian food in the country. After Birmingham."

I thought quickly. This could be useful. "Oh Alex – I'm sorry, I can't go out that night. I promised to go and see my mum. But I could always come along to the match first."

"OK, fine," he said easily, betraying no disappointment even though he was probably hoping we'd get together as usual. "Come along for the game and then I'll drop you at the station."

And that's exactly what happened. We all piled into the two cars, Alex's and Sam's. Holly was there, and Sam's friend William from the radio station, as well as Sarah, Jake and Amy from the office.

It was fun. I even began to feel sorry. At last I'd found friends who accepted me, who didn't think of me as plain and awkward and strange. I'd learned to relax a little, to laugh and joke and not take things so seriously. And with my new confidence I'd found my own style, a look I was happy with. I'd come a long way in a very short time.

But the sad thing was, this new life just wasn't enough for me. I'd seen what I really wanted: James. And that meant that soon, very soon, I'd be saying goodbye to all this . . .

The game was pretty exciting, especially for me. Middleton was considered to be a powerful match for Dudlace – better established and on the verge of entering the league. Several commentators had already predicted they'd be in by the following year. You could tell that the local fans thought Dudlace would be a pushover. In fact, they gave the impression that their team was slumming it by even bothering.

So our sense of triumph when we beat them hollow was even sweeter. And for me it was just the beginning of what I knew would be a magical day, a turning point in my whole life. Because the undoubted hero of the hour, the player of the day, the man of the match, was none other than James Angel – the man of my dreams, the man destined to be mine. And in just a few short hours, I'd be in his arms once again, just as I was always meant to be.

So it was with an edge of joy that I cheered along with the others, thrilling to the tight control of the forward formation, rejoicing in James's powerful frame, his almost warrior-like attack once the ball was in his grasp and the goal within his distance.

Three times he had the chance, and three times he sent the ball scudding into goal, once even sending it deftly right through the splayed legs of the goalie, much to the delight of our crowd. We leaped up and down, yelling, whistling, hooting, with excitement and pride.

It was a massive victory and a thorough humiliation of a far more seasoned side. The Middleton fans were silenced when the final whistle blew. They'd been trounced 4–1 by a little team they'd obviously thought were nothing. And we'd been there to see it all.

We jostled out of the grounds and made our way to the main street where we all piled into a little café and ordered steaming cups of hot chocolate and sticky cakes. Everyone was laughing and joking, intoxicated with our brilliant win.

"I wish you didn't have to go," Alex said when I got up to leave. "Can't you go to your mum's tomorrow?"

I shook my head regretfully, genuinely sorry to leave everyone.

"I'd like to – but I promised, and it's her birthday," I improvised.

"I'll run you to the station," he offered.

"Don't be silly," I said lightly. "It's just down the road from here. You stay and have another drink. I'll be fine."

I slipped away and made my way down the High Street, clutching my overnight case. It was five-thirty, which gave me about an hour and a half to kill before my big moment. I knew James's routine well enough to realize that at this very moment he was probably being interviewed by excited journalists, anxious to herald their newfound hero. Then he'd probably spend a bit of time with the rest of the team. Then a shower and rest before his girlfriend showed up, any time after seven.

Only tonight, it would be a different girlfriend. The real one. Me.

I faltered for a moment, realizing I'd been walking the wrong way. What I needed was a nice big anonymous shop. I knew that there was a branch of Teeton's, a huge department store, but I'd misread my map. There it was, right at the other end of the High Street.

I turned round and walked the other way, past the café where I was sure everyone was still huddled, engrossed in their conversation, probably yet another blow by blow argument about exactly how Middleton had come to lose quite so badly today. I walked quickly by, caught up in a swirl of late afternoon shoppers. Looking straight ahead, I forced myself not to glance through the café window.

To my relief, Teeton's was open till six-thirty. I slipped inside and glided up the escalator to the first floor – ladies' fashions. I picked three or four impossibly expensive outfits from the rails and spent a happy half-hour trying them on and imagining being rich enough to own them.

After that, I simply changed into the smart, sexy little dress I'd brought with me, and bundled my daytime things into the overnight bag. I made my way up another floor to the ladies, did my make-up and brushed my hair. I looked good. I knew I did. The dress clung to my slim figure and tiny waist, revealing just the right hint of cleavage at the point where the low neckline buttoned. The unfamiliar black high-heels made me look older – more poised and sexy.

My face was flushed with the healthy outdoor glow of the day, mingled with a heady night-time excitement. I added some blusher to my cheekbones and applied a new plum-coloured lipstick that made my mouth look full and sensual.

A bell rang to indicate that the store was closing. I made my way back down the escalators to the ground floor perfume hall. As I walked through, I helped myself to a generous spray of the most expensive one, and stalked out of the shop in a haze of unbelievable luxury and style.

That left half an hour. I consulted my street map. The Clarendon Hotel was a good twenty-minute walk from the High Street. I set off, my heart singing. I was ready now, ready to make the gesture that would win me back the man I loved – or lose him for ever. But right now, I wasn't scared. I felt confident, beautiful, unbeatable. Men were looking at me admiringly as I went by.

It wasn't until I'd swung through the imposing revolving doors of the hotel that I began to feel my first misgivings. The lobby was huge, polished, very quiet and almost oppressively luxurious. There were white sofas on white rugs, sparkling glass coffee tables and marble pillars everywhere. It was the most intimidating place I'd ever seen.

A couple of uniformed doormen gave me long glances as I flounced past them. A receptionist behind the vast white and gold desk smiled a welcome. I certainly didn't want anyone checking whether I was a resident or who I was coming to see, so I just carried on walking until I reached a bar. A few people were there sipping things like double whiskies and Campari and soda. I ordered a glass of wine just for courage.

No one took any notice of me as I sat at my table. That was exactly what I wanted. I got my bearings, drained my drink and walked through the back of the bar and out into a corridor. My hunch had been right. This was a different route to the back of the hotel. I carried on walking until I found a pair of elevators. Then I pressed the button, my stomach now a cavern of butterflies as I drew nearer and nearer to my destiny.

OK, this is it, I told myself as the hotel lift glided to the fourth floor. Peering in the tactfully lit mirrors that lined the imposing, sweet-smelling elevator, I saw that my eyes were glittering and my cheeks unnaturally flushed. My face was displaying all the ragged emotions that churned inside me – fear and excitement, triumph and anxiety, hope and despair.

Silently, the golden doors slid open and I was in a long, richly-carpeted corridor with paintings on the walls and the occasional bronze statue on marble stands. I adjusted my smart black dress, specially bought for the occasion. It was tight round my newly chiselled waist, the neck line plunging. I was wearing nothing underneath it. Nothing at all.

It seemed to take for ever to pace down the elegantly curved hallway, past door after door, until I reached number 42. And then, at last, I was there in front of it, the brightly-polished number glinting at me. Was it encouraging me to knock, daring me to throw all my dreams in the air? And if I did, would they come true, or would they all come crashing down, breaking into little pieces like my heart?

Three times I lifted my trembling arm, my fingers clenched into a fist, poised to knock. Three times I hesitated, then dropped my wrist back down again. It was such a momentous event, this – the culmination of all my plans and all my careful scheming. No wonder that now the moment of truth was just seconds away, I was breathless with terror, almost unable to act.

I took a couple of deep breaths, and tried to get a grip on

166

the turbulent feelings storming inside me. Then, at last, I forced myself to knock on the door. I composed my face into a bright smile, patted my wild hair nervously, smoothed down the dress again so that it covered at least some of my thighs, and waited. I heard a movement behind the door. Transfixed, I began to wonder whether I could bear the suspense.

Then the door opened and it all began to come true. There was James, my James, looking as fabulous as ever, his strong frame emphasized by the open-necked blue shirt, the tight-fitting jeans. His face was wreathed in a wide, welcoming smile.

It was for me. All for me. Just as I'd planned it, just exactly as I'd imagined it through all those long, lonely weeks away from him.

Seventeen

"Hello, James," I said, when he opened the door. "It's me. It really is me. And now at last we can be together again, just as we were meant to be . . ."

Even as I forced out the words I'd rehearsed so often I knew something was wrong. They were falling like stones between us, unheard, certainly not understood. James's face, which moments before had been so warm and welcoming, was now transformed into a mask of horror and disbelief. He looked haunted, and I was his ghost.

"Katie, I can't believe this," he said at last. But there was no joy in his words. "I thought you'd given up all this madness."

"Don't call it that," I begged, still clinging to any hope I could that I might be able to get through to him, to make him see sense. Somehow, I managed to squeeze past him and into the bedroom. He didn't exactly bar my way, but just stood helplessly watching me as I sat down in an armchair by the bed.

"But Charlotte told me—" he began to say.

"Oh, yes," I cut in, my voice dangerous with venom now that the hateful name had been uttered. "What exactly did she tell you? What lies has she been cooking up about me to turn you against me? Because I know, James, I know far more than you think. I know she's just trying to come between us—"

"Stop it!" James yelled at me, slamming his fists into his ears. "This is crazy, Katie, you must see that. You and I – it's over. It was finished before I met Charlotte. She had nothing to do with it."

A terrible coldness was creeping over my heart. James was in deadly earnest, there was no mistaking it. The look he was giving me was enough to tell me that. There was no love in it, only disgust and a vague pity.

"But . . ." I faltered, clinging to the last tiny fragment of hope. "But I love you so much, James. We had such good times together. Surely you can see I'm better for you than her. I understand—"

"You don't know what you're saying," James muttered, clearly at a loss for what to do. "I never loved you, Katie. I kept trying to explain. You're gorgeous and you were sweet and we had some fun. But that was nothing. With Charlotte, I've got something really special."

I couldn't bear to hear the tenderness in his voice. It

pierced me like a sword. But somehow I couldn't stop, either. "She – she's not your type," I whispered.

"How would you know what my type is?" spat James scornfully.

"She doesn't understand football," I pointed out. "She doesn't even like it. She doesn't understand stardom or the life of an international player. She – she doesn't even like staying in fancy hotels. She can't keep up with you, not like I can."

James's eyes narrowed. "You're just kidding yourself, Katie. You don't even know me. You may know about football, but why should that matter to me? And as for Charlotte, what do you know about her?"

"You'd be surprised," I said, unable to keep a note of menace out of my voice.

"Charlotte said she'd met you," he said slowly. "She said you'd promised to keep away from me. She believed you. She even made me believe you. She said I should feel sorry for you. But she was wrong, wasn't she?"

"She was coming between us," I insisted, my words sounding hollow even to me by now. "I – I wanted to bring you to your senses. That's why I'm here instead of her. To show you where you really belong."

"Wait a moment," James said, moving towards me with a sudden note of fear in his voice. "Where is she, then? Where's

170

Charlotte? And – and how did you know she didn't want to stay in a hotel? What's going on, Katie? Tell me now!"

Suddenly he was looming over me, firing out his questions with a mounting urgency. I was scared. Scared of James, and scared of what I'd done.

"She's – she's gone to meet you," I whispered. "I – I sent her. So that I could come here and be alone with you."

"Where?" thundered James. He was furious now. His hands were gripping the tops of my arms as he forced me to stand up. "Where did you send her? What on earth did you think you were doing?"

Trembling with fear, I told him what I'd done and where she was. His eyes were wide with disbelief.

"You really are crazy," he said. "No, you're worse than that. You're – you're evil." As he spoke, he pulled on a jacket, then stopped to scribble down the address I gave him.

"See yourself out," he snapped, not even bothering to look at me as he barged through the door. "I'm going to find her. I've got to find her . . ."

It was as though he was talking to himself. As though I wasn't even there, too insignificant to bother to hate. Clearly all that mattered to him was Charlotte. And I was nothing. Nothing at all.

For a while I just sat in the armchair, too stunned and broken-hearted to move. After what might have been hours, or maybe just a few minutes, I looked round me. This was the room where James was planning to spend the night with Charlotte, the woman he loved. Get used to it. *Get used to it. He loves her, not you.*

On a little table by the window was a bottle of champagne in an ice bucket. There were two glasses – for the lovers, James and Charlotte. I wanted to get up and leave, go home and bury myself in my misery, but somehow I couldn't. I just wanted a little while longer to be part of this world, this dream. For I knew now what I'd never dared admit before: James was only a dream to me and our love affair was a fantasy. The real one had ended weeks ago. The rest was all in my mind.

Sadly, I opened the bottle. It made a joyous little pop. I poured a glass of the bubbling wine and began to sip it, trying to draw comfort from its sweet-sour fizz. And it did give me a kind of comfort. My head began to feel lighter, the pain in my heart just a little less piercing. So I poured myself another glass and sat on the bed, imagining how wonderful this would have felt if it had been the two of us, clinking glasses, downing champagne as we gazed into each other's eyes. If only he loved me as I loved him!

Just a few minutes more I promised myself, pouring another glass. Then I'd have to return to my drab life, a life without James. But for the moment, in this gilded setting, drinking the fizzy, celebratory drink of lovers, I wanted to stay here and dream.

Of course, by this time I was feeling rather strange. I'd almost finished the bottle all by myself. My cheeks felt flushed and my head was spinning gently. I lay down on the bed, clutching the pillow for comfort, and drifted into sleep.

And then the phone rang. Blearily, I lifted it.

"Call for James Angel," said the hotel receptionist. "Can I put the caller through?"

And before I had a chance to speak, I heard a different voice – Charlotte's frantic tones, echoing strangely.

"Hello – hello, is that James?" she asked impatiently. "Listen, the line's really bad, I'm on the mobile. There's no phone in this stupid cottage."

"Hello, Charlotte," I said wearily.

There was a pause. "Who's that?" she asked suspiciously.

"It's Katie," I told her. What else could I say? There seemed little point in deceiving her now. "James's not here."

"Well, what are you doing there?" she demanded. "And where is he?"

"He's probably on his way to Greenacres," I suggested.

"Greenacres! How did you know where I was?" Silence. "Katie – oh God, I can't believe this! Don't tell me you're up to your mad tricks again. I thought there was something funny about that letter but I knew there was no way I could

173

contact James until after the match, so I couldn't phone to check until now. Listen, I'm coming over there right now. I don't believe a word you're saying but just stay there."

I wanted to tell her she could believe me, that it would be better to stay and wait for James, but she didn't give me a chance and she certainly wasn't going to trust me. In fact, every ten minutes she rang from the car to check that I was still there.

About an hour later she burst into the room, looking round wildly.

"Where is he?" she wanted to know. "The truth, Katie. Where's James?"

I shrugged. "I told you. He's gone to the cottage to find you. You should have listened to me."

"Well, if you're telling the truth he'll get there, see my note, and come straight back here," she said shortly. "And while we're waiting, perhaps you'd like to tell me exactly what you've been up to. I just can't wait to hear."

But I didn't get a chance to tell her, because at that very moment there was a knock on the door and a strange man entered. He was middle-aged, with a very red, outdoor complexion, thinning hair and hard, strong-looking muscles. Football muscles. He was breathless, as if he'd been running. And his face was strained with anxiety and shock.

"Which one of you is Charlotte?" he asked, getting straight to the point.

"I am," Charlotte told him, suddenly fearful. "Why? What's going on?"

"James's in hospital, love," he said. "I'm Tim Praeger, the team manager. I just heard. He's been in a road accident and he's been rushed to Dudlace General. I'm off there myself – and I thought you'd want to be there too."

"How badly is he hurt?" Charlotte asked, her face white and crumpled. "Is he – is he going to be OK?"

"I don't know, love," Tim said. "I just don't know."

And then they were gone. James's rightful girlfriend, the girl he loved, was flying off to be by his side. And I was left alone, abandoned, forgotten, while the very thought of James in hospital, fighting for his life, suffering terrible injuries, was tearing me apart. It wasn't only that I was worried about him, though that was bad enough. Even worse was the gut-wrenching realization that this accident would never have happened if it hadn't been for me. I'd driven him out into the night and now he was gone – possibly even dead.

Somehow, I had to get to the hospital and find out what had happened. I had to know the worst, even as I prayed he was going to be all right. He might hate me, despise me, wish I'd never come into his life, but I still loved him. And how could I live with myself now, knowing what I'd done?

Eighteen

Numb with misery, I finally dragged myself out of James's room and slouched back down that rich, carpeted corridor. Only a short while ago I'd bounced along that same hallway with such a confident spring in my step. Now my shoulders were bowed, my legs felt like lead, my head was lolling practically to my chest I felt so ashamed, so awful.

I was so lost in my own bleak thoughts, my eyes focused on the floor, that I would never have recognized the familiar figure that greeted me as I emerged from the lift. I wouldn't have noticed him at all, if he hadn't called out my name and strode over to grasp my arm.

"Katie! Hey, Katie – what on earth's the matter with you?"

"Alex!" I exclaimed, startled and at the same time overjoyed to see him. Alex would know what to do. Alex would help out and make everything all right, the way he always did. "What – what are you doing here?"

Alex grinned – not quite his usual open smile but a wry look tinged with tension. "I could ask you the same thing," he replied grimly. "Whatever happened to having to get home to Mummy?"

I blushed, and found I couldn't reply.

"Tell you what," he suggested. "Why don't you let me get you a drink and you can tell me all about it over a bowl of incredibly overpriced peanuts."

"No!" I shouted, so loudly that several very smart people in evening dress turned to sneer at me. "No – I mean, I can't. You don't understand. I have to get over to the hospital right away. It's James."

"Yes, I had a feeling it might be," Alex commented drily. "Well, I know when I'm not needed . . ."

"Oh, but you are!" I blurted out. "Listen, James Angel's in hospital in Dudlace and – and it's all my fault. He may be badly hurt. He may even be . . ." I gulped, choked down a sob, then carried on: "It may be really serious. I've got to find out, Alex. Please help me."

Alex gave me a strange look – almost cold, certainly not friendly. Then he shrugged. "I'll take you if you want. I happen to be going that way – for the second time in a day. Quite a treat."

"The second time!" I echoed, puzzled. "Why?"

"I'll tell you my story if you tell me yours," he said. "But I'm warning you, mine isn't very pretty. And yours, from the sound of it, is going to be even uglier."

So as we made our way through the darkening streets and out to the open country road, we made our confessions. Alex's was very simple.

"I know you must think I'm just a fool," he told me. "I mean, you've been stringing me along all these weeks, haven't you? Knowing that I was falling in love with you—"

"No!" I burst in. "I didn't know that. I thought we were just friends, taking it slowly, getting to know each other."

Alex laughed harshly. "Think that if you want, Katie, but you're pretty good at kidding yourself if you believe it. What were all those kisses, and more than kisses? All the times you came on hot, then cold. Responded to me then pushed me away. You wanted me; you know you did."

I was silent, knowing that he was right. At times I had wanted Alex and I'd known in my heart that he was getting serious about me, whatever he said. But it hadn't suited me to believe that. I realized I was very good at believing exactly what I wanted, never mind what happened to be true.

"But I'm not quite the fool you took me for," Alex went on. "I knew there was something wrong, something in the way between us. And it didn't take a genius to work out that it must be another guy. I didn't want to think you were foolish enough to be carrying a candle for James Angel, though. That came as quite a shock."

"How did you find out?" I asked faintly.

"It was hard not to, in the end," Alex sighed. "Little hints here, little details there. Every time we went to a Dudlace match I noticed how you were, watching him on the field. And how distant you were to me afterwards. I saw you addressing envelopes to him a while back, making the odd phone call. Oh, don't worry, I wasn't spying on you, not intentionally. But my desk is quite close to yours, you know . . ."

"So why did you carry on seeing me?" I asked, embarrassed but curious at the same time. "I mean, if you knew I was still involved with James."

"That was the point," Alex said patiently. "The fact is, I knew you weren't. Everyone knew you and James had finished. We'd all seen him with his new girlfriend. I mean, you had yourself. Not that that means very much, given the number of girls James Angel gets through in a month. I just knew that you weren't going out with him and I thought you'd work through your crush on him if I just hung around. So then, when you said you needed another couple of weeks, I thought that was your deadline for getting over him. And then we might have had a chance together . . ."

I winced at his words. "Might have had a chance" sounded

very final.

"I suppose in a way that was exactly what I'd done," I admitted. "I wanted to see James alone one more time to see if I could get him back. And I guess I wanted you to be there."

"As second best," Alex said bitterly. "How flattering. Is that why you decided to lie to me?"

I didn't reply. I was feeling too ashamed.

"Because that's what hurt the most, Katie," he went on quietly. "You were crazy to cling on to a silly fantasy about James Angel being your boyfriend. No one can really help the way they feel, but we can all do something about how we behave to other people. And lying to someone who cares about you just isn't on."

"I'm sorry," I whispered. "Really I am. But – I didn't want to hurt you."

Alex snorted. "Oh, I see. It was all for me, was it? That's nice. It was very nice to see you sneaking past the café five minutes after you'd left to go and see your mum. As if I'd believed that little story in the first place, considering you've never found a good thing to say about her on the rare occasions when you even mention her! I should think you'd rather spend a wet weekend at White Hart Lane than any time at all with her."

"So you did see me," I breathed, beginning to understand.

"Yes, I saw you. And I had a feeling you'd got a hot little

date – or thought you had. And don't get me wrong, Katie, I wasn't interested in spoiling it for you. I just wanted to know for sure what kind of girl I was getting tangled up with. I wanted to see for myself whether my suspicions were true. So I worked out where James was staying, which wasn't difficult because the TV was blaring in the café – a full-length interview with him at the Clarendon Hotel."

"But what have you been doing between then and now?" It was now nearly nine o'clock, over three hours since he'd seen me outside the café.

"I had a car full of friends depending on me for a lift," he reminded me. "We thought about staying on in Middleton but in the end everyone wanted to go home so I drove them and then came back. I thought I'd find you eventually. And I'd only been waiting an hour or so when you arrived – looking, if I may say so, not exactly like a girl with a hot date. Very like a girl without one."

I burst into tears. Then, between sobs, I blurted out exactly what I'd done. How I'd persuaded myself that Charlotte was the wrong girl for James, how I'd followed her round finding out everything I could about her. And then, when we saw Great Aunt Judy's cottage just a few days ago, how I'd hatched my plot to get her out of the way so that I could be with James again, just the way I'd dreamed it would happen.

"Interesting," Alex commented coldly. "I really enjoyed that day out. It made me think it was worth hanging on because I thought I was with the real Katie, the fun one, the genuine one. And all along you were just using me for your little scheme. Well, thanks a lot for trampling on another memory!"

"It wasn't like that," I protested. "Honestly, I enjoyed it too. I liked you. I mean – I do like you, Alex."

"Shame, that," Alex said, "because I don't think I like you much, Katie. I've realized there isn't anything much left to like."

I wanted to cry then, to weep and to beg him to give me another chance. I couldn't bear his coldness and his disgust. But there was no time for that. I had to get to the hospital and I had to tell him why.

So I carried on with my story until I reached the very moment when Charlotte was whisked off to James's bedside and I was left alone, frantic with worry and grief and overwhelmed with guilt.

"Because it's all my fault," I burst out. "Whatever happens now, James's accident is all because of me."

And I was in such anguish that Alex must have felt sorry for me despite everything. He reached over and squeezed my arm.

"No, it's not your fault, Katie. James was driving. You weren't there. It was nothing to do with you."

And although I didn't believe him, his kind words

consoled me just a little and made me strong enough to face the next terrible ordeal: the hospital.

Alex dropped me off outside and gave me a cold little wave before pulling away from the kerb. I felt terribly abandoned and alone as I made my way past the ambulances and stretchers and late-night visitors, up to the reception desk to ask where James was.

It took a while to persuade the nurse on duty even to tell me which floor he was on. I suppose they had to be careful about the press and all his fans. And after all, I wasn't a relative. I wasn't even a friend. That cruel truth was boring into me like a nail hammering into my heart. I wasn't his girlfriend. I wasn't anything to him.

But somehow, maybe because my face was so stricken with grief, the nurse relented and eventually led me through a maze of echoing corridors and staircases to a little waiting area. Tim Praeger was sitting there, his head in his hands. And so was Charlotte.

'What are you doing here?" she snarled at once. "Haven't you done enough damage for one night?"

"I – I'm sorry, Charlotte," I said as meekly as I could. "I really am. I'm sorry for everything. I just needed to know how James is."

"We don't know, love," Tim said kindly, sensing the urgency in my voice. "He had a nasty collision with a heavy goods vehicle. He's concussed quite badly and there's a couple of broken ribs and a lot of bruising. But until he regains consciousness we won't know how serious it is."

"He means, we don't know if he's brain-damaged," snapped Charlotte. She was obviously terribly shocked, and seeing me was about the last thing she needed.

"I don't want to intrude," I whispered, forcing myself to carry on, "but I just have to know he's OK."

"Why? What are you to him?" Charlotte retaliated, her white face streaked with tears. "Can't you get it into your thick head, he doesn't want you in his life? OK?"

I gulped. "I know that," I said softly. "He loves you, he really does. You mean the world to him."

"Did he tell you that?" Charlotte demanded, interested despite herself.

I nodded. "You're all he cares about. I should never have tried to get in the way or rake up a past that never was. I was wrong, I see that now. And I'm truly sorry."

Charlotte's face softened. "Well, I think you are," she said at last. "But you're still a silly cow. And you've done some pretty vile things."

"I know," I said. "I wish I could turn back the clock – I wish I'd never done any of it. It was so obvious that he's crazy about you. You should have seen the way he rushed after you. I don't understand why he seemed so – so frantic."

"Oh, that's James all over," Charlotte's voice was suddenly tender. "He worries far too much about me. I'm a diabetic, you see, and he always worries that I'm going to be stranded somewhere without my insulin. As if I'd be stupid enough to go anywhere without it . . ."

Suddenly, a whole lot of details began to fall into place. Charlotte hadn't been a picky eater. She hadn't been madly dieting to be thin and glamorous. She was a diabetic who had to watch what she ate or she'd be seriously ill. No wonder James was alarmed at the idea of her stuck in the middle of nowhere, in the middle of the night.

For a while we fell silent, all three of us willing James to be well, to get better. *Please don't die! Please don't die!* It was then that those words kept pounding through my head like a drum, my whole being aching with dread and anguish.

After what seemed like an eternity, a grave-looking doctor appeared from the swing doors that led to James's room. He approached Charlotte.

"He's regained consciousness," he told her, "and he's asking for you. I must warn you not to let him get over-excited. Just spend a few minutes with him. He's going to be fine, but right now he's still very fragile."

I had to watch as Charlotte, weeping with relief, was led through the doors to the man who loved her more than anything on earth. I had to bury my own tears of relief and anguish, knowing I had no right to feel anything. Quietly, I crept to the doors and, on tiptoes, peered through the glass. Charlotte was sitting by the bed, holding James's hand. His head was swathed in bandages and he was very pale, but there was no mistaking the look of adoration on his face as he gazed into her eyes.

As I watched them, I realized I'd never felt so alone in my whole life. Slowly, I crept back past the little waiting area, Tim's kind eyes following me as I made my way down the long, shiny, forbidding corridors.

As I left the hospital, I saw a familiar car waiting outside, a familiar face inside.

"What are you doing here?" I asked Alex for the second time that evening. "I thought you'd never speak to me again."

Alex didn't answer at first. "How's James?" he asked, and I told him.

"That's good," he nodded. Then, without another word, he drove me home.

He pulled up outside my door, then turned to look at me seriously.

"Katie, I'm sorry for everything. Sorry for what you've been through. Sorry things haven't worked out."

"We could try again," I said between my tears, suddenly wanting more than anything to be back with Alex, just the way it was.

He shook his head. "No, we couldn't. It's too late for that. But I do want to start liking you again, Katie. I want to start knowing you properly – the real Katie, I mean, not all those people you've been pretending to be."

"I want that too," I told him shyly. "I've made so many mistakes."

"The important thing about mistakes," Alex said, "is to learn from them. Goodnight, Katie."

And then I was really alone. And, although it was going to take me a long, long time to come to terms with all the foolish, dangerous, cruel things I'd done, I felt in a strange way as though I'd been given a lifeline. Alex wanted to believe in me, and that made me want to believe in myself.

So now, right now, I was going to start proving to us both that I had it in me to begin all over again – a stronger, more honest person. But a person with a past.